Surrender

Surrender

Gabrielle St. Charles

ISBN 0-9701823-0-9

Surrender

Many thanks to those of you, who sat by me in spirit day in and day out. I truly appreciate all that you have led me to do. I have written since I was seven years old and with the inspiration of God and the help of my friends, I have no truly become an author. For my daughter, whom has sat and played with everything in the house, knowing that I had no idea what she was doing...someday you children will do the same to you. She is my inspiration in my life. I was truly blessed when she came into my life. I hope that I do her justice in her education, her creativity, her athleticism and her open-mindedness.

It is frustrating to see so many of my friends ostracized by churches, families, friends and other communities. It is my hope and dream that we all come to know ourselves and that the judgment that is so readily thrust upon us, is, instead left to us and our Higher Power. If you can live your life honestly and find peaceful existence, you are doing the right thing. I hope one day my mother reads this and knows that I do love God with all my heart and all my soul and that I try and do the right thing, but I can't do what I am not capable of doing. This works comes to you not through me, but through inspiration much higher than I. My gift is from God and I hope you enjoy my works. My true dedication of this work is to my father, Charlie, who was my first love in life. My unconditional love that still exists, even though he was killed. And, to my little brother, my best friend...He sat by me in illness and let me know that it would get better. He and my father sit together and probably fish all day long. If there are fishing holes in heaven. I love you both dearly...and I know you sit close by in the hard times.

Thank you for your love.

Chapter 1

My Harley felt good underneath me. I found that riding fast and free made me feel so much better. I had gotten a call from Maria; it was the usual. She had about two hours and wanted me to meet her at our spot. I had jumped at the chance.

I never thought I would be the type of woman, who, at thirty-five, would drop anything for another woman. But, she was different. She couldn't embarrass her parents and our relationship had to remain a secret.

I had been seeing her for almost six months now and she was able to spend a few nights at my house, or we would meet for dinner, sneak out to a secluded part or our favorite pond. That's where I was headed now. She was so beautiful. I remembered so much about here when she was absent. I remembered how her hair fell on my shoulders and my arm when she nuzzled into me and laid her head on my chest. The smell of her air aroused me deep inside. She had the softest, wavy, thick, dark brown hair. Spanish ancestry had been good to her; she had the look and class of a queen. Her distinction belied the fact that her family was dirt-poor hard workers who couldn't get out of poverty.

She didn't mind. She had her Lord, her loved ones and most of all she had me. When she met me at the library, she stared for at least a half-hour. I noticed her watching me, never moving. Finally I went to her, knowing that she was too young for me, knowing that there was no way she was a lesbian, but I went over to her anyway. Our conversation had been short. I had asked if there was something wrong.

I remembered her words vividly, "No. You are beautiful and I can't quit looking at you. I hope you aren't offended."

My heart lightened immediately. I hadn't minded at all. My words back to her were, "No, I don't mind at all, if you would like to meet me for dinner later, I would love it."

She accepted and we went for our first date that evening. Since then, we had spent time on the phone, met at odd times and just gotten to know each other. We had an instant rapport and I taught her what it was like to know a woman: I was her first.

The highway sped beneath me, the wind blowing my dark hair against my shoulders around my leather jacket. It was kind of chilling going this fast and I pulled my jacket closed and the zipper up a little higher. I could hardly wait to see her, my excitement peaking each time I thought of her.

Maria's parents had been having a hard time with Maria's younger sister, Monica. Because of that, Maria had to do a lot of the work around the house and care for the six other children, all under that age of twelve. Her family was very close-knit and it was exceptionally important to her parents for them to all be home so that Monica had a true sense of belonging. So, it was up to Maria to stay at home and her parents were so suspicious of everything they did due to Monica's lies and deceit. We just had to ride it out Maria said; it would just be a matter of time before she had her freedom back.

She was brilliant, Maria. She had worked her way through school until this year, when one of her professors had approached her and asked if she would accept a scholarship that allowed her to financially complete school. The scholarship provided almost a full-ride and she had called me the night she found out and we celebrated; she snuck out. She asked me to meet her at an out-of-the way restaurant.

When I arrived, she had surprised me with the fact that no one else was in the place. No staff and no customers, we had the place all to ourselves. Her friend, Tony, owned the business and let her use it on their day off, so they were closed. She had made us dinner and later that night; we made love for the first time. It was fabulous. I had memories of that night ingrained in my brain. Of her seducing me to the jukebox music, the dessert she had made, fresh strawberries and a sugary cream, dipped and dripped all over her as she had seductively undressed, little by little...dripping the cream down her breasts as she watched my reaction. She let me lick it off, finally feeding me the strawberry. I hadn't been able to control myself. I made love to her right there...and surprisingly enough, she made love to me too.

She was skilled for her first time. She followed my every move and when I had inquired about it later, to her element of skill, she said she just did to me what she had dreamed of wanting me to do to her for months as she lay in bed at night. After that, we snuck away for whole nights. Not often, but it was well worth the wait. She was so sexy and so seductive. Her hot-blooded passion was nothing like her easy demeanor by day. It was like day and night, her wanton passion unleashed in my bed.

I pulled my bike into the crest of trees, knowing I would probably be there before she got there. I loved sitting and waiting for her to come down the path. She walked with such grace and charm, most of what I liked about her, the air she exuded. And, I loved seeing her light up when she saw me. I knew that she would be thinking of me and that finally I had found someone who felt as I did, I did not doubt her love for me.

She never hid her feelings. When she was mad, she let me have it. When she was unhappy, she shared with me the reasons and when she wanted to make love to me, she definitely let me know. The look in her eyes as honest and pure as were her other emotions. No one had ruined her yet.

I cherished my time with her. When we were apart, I would work and spend time with friends, but my mind and my heart never left her. I wondered what she was doing, what her life that she couldn't share with me was like and at times I felt myself falling into her, but knew I had to keep my head above water and not let myself fall for her. Her parents couldn't handle her being a lesbian.

One night we talked about her 'problem' being a lesbian. She told me she could never come out of the closet; never have the dream of being married to me, of having children with me, sharing that with her family. Her cousin, Jaime, was gay. The family had been shamed, disgraced, overwhelmed. She had watched and listened, knowing she was taking their judgment just as he was. She even watched his parents kick him out of the family; they no longer welcomed him as part of their own. Jaime had been so distraught about losing his place in his family that he became promiscuous. Later that year, he found out he had AIDS. Aunt Rosina still wouldn't let him back in the family, because he was a disgrace and now he was being paid back with the disease of homosexuals.

Maria had been devastated. She had known that she was a lesbian from the time she was eight, and now she knew that to bare that truth to them she would lose them. Jaime died alone, without family. Not even Maria was allowed to see him- that would deface the family. There were eight children in her family and she was the eldest. If she outed herself and lost the relationship with the siblings it would kill her. They were like her very own and she couldn't have them think bad things of her. She had cried to me about how much she loved and that we would never have more than we did now- a few nights snuck away, a few meeting throughout the week and nothing like she wanted with me.

I just listened. I knew that one day she would surrender to her passion and either leave her family or leave me. One of the other would have to happen. I knew she felt as I did, we shared our love, and that there would never be another woman who compared to her in my life. She was bright, intelligent, articulate, compassionate, caring, loving, seductive, playful, savvy and classy and as much as I hated to admit it, I was in love with her.

Even I knew I couldn't hide it long enough to fool myself. If she could live like this, then I could too. I would wait until she left me for her family. Just sharing what we had now was enough. Sometimes I was confident our love would succumb, that it would win out, that it would be enough; other times, I didn't think love was near enough. I wish I didn't go back and forth so much, I thought.

I loved her enough that I could give her up for her family when the time came. That much I knew.

I saw her break onto the path and my face immediately spread into a permanent grin, one she drew out of me so easily. She saw me as I saw her and she ran to me. I was still on my bike and she climbed right on in front of me, straddling the cycle and I at the same time. I kissed her, my lips tearing at hers in hunger. I pulled her as close as I could as if to say that we were one, to meld to her. I kissed her neck, behind her ear and heard her whisper.

"Shane..." she was hoarse, barely audible.

"I love you, Baby." I kissed her again.

My lips softer, expressing my love for her without hunger this time. With my hands on her back, I softly cradled her.

"Here, let me take off my jacket, you have to be chilled." She helped me with it and slid it on.

"I love wearing this. It always smells just like you." She smiled as she sniffed it and then sniffed just at my collarbone.

On the nights that we got together, when we would ride, she would tell me how much she loved it and wrap up both up in it as the wind hit us; I liked to ride fast.

I wondered why I was here, how she got time away. Did she have a little extra time? Maybe something special had happened? Maybe nothing at all...It was my time with her and I cherished it, every minute I got to spend. I tipped my head to hers and touched her forehead with mine. We called it our 'meeting of the minds.' She had come up with it one night after we made love; she laid her forehead on mine and told me that we never had to speak words again, because we could just lay our heads together and know what the other was thinking. It was a nice concept. Many times we would get frustrated at not being able to spend much time together and we would have a 'meeting of the minds' and just relish in the few moments we got together.

She laid her forehead softly against mine and I started to

calm. Something was on her mind, I could tell. I hated to ruin our time though, so I said nothing.

We stayed like that for some time, before she said anything and then quietly she broke our silence. "I have an offer to study abroad. I got it today."

"What exactly does that mean for you?"

She took a deep breath, "Well, I would spend six months in Europe at different hospitals studying under Dr. Walter Laird." She pulled me closer.

Wow! That was out of the blue. It was bad enough not to see her for a couple of days, let alone six months. I had to be supportive though. I refused to let my disappointment ruin her good news.

"Baby, that's wonderful."

Her career was as important to her as mine was to me. We were driven women and she supported me so much, even the nights when she had to put up with my working late, while she was there. Being an attorney wasn't all it was cracked up to be. The research alone was devastating to my time, but when I was working on a case like the one I had when I first met her, I spent fifteen plus hours a day working. That is how I met her, researching in the library for the case I was prosecuting.

"But, I won't see you. I can't go that long without seeing you, Shane. I can't do it. I don't want to do it. And, with Monica being so rebellious, how will Mama handle it? It's not good timing." She laid her head on my shoulder and sighed heavily.

"There, there...Sweetness, it's okay. I'm sure we can talk this out; let's look at it rationally. Can we do that?" I pulled her away from my shoulder and cradled her face. "Can we do that?"

She wouldn't look at me. She had her eyes closed tightly and wouldn't look at me.

"Please look at me, Sweetie. Please?"

She kissed me hard and passionately, never opening her eyes, prodding me to explore with her depths charged by our electricity. She pried my lips open and dove into my mouth, seeking my tongue. Her hands roved my back, scratching faintly with her nails. I was just as hungry and reflected that in my touch and my kiss. It had been more than a week since we had gotten anything but the phone. Finally, she gave up and pulled away, it must not have made her stop thinking. I knew that is what she wanted from her actions, to just make it all go away and to savor the moment. She thought too much, she was a worrier; it made her crazy.

She spoke, husky and raspy, "You're so beautiful, Shane. So...so beautiful. I don't want to be away from you anymore than I am now. I lay awake at night and I think of you. I want you...I want us." She was intense.

I didn't know what to do, but I knew she has been in thought about this sometime by the look in her eyes, searching me, drawing out some kind of answer. Maybe she just couldn't make a decision?

"Wanna go for a ride?" sometimes that helped. At least I could suggest it.

"Yeah. Let's just cruise the pond slowly."

It was our favorite thing to do, just cruise around the lake slowly and she could hold onto me in public without it being reckoned with. She would talk to me as we rode, in my ear, whispering sometimes and sometimes making lude comments as we inched forward.

I didn't know how much time we had. Sometimes it was just an hour or so. I would much rather take her home, to my house.

"No, the pond is too close to my house. Can we just go home?" She asked.

"Do we have enough time?" I let it draw out slowly; hoping but not hoping so much I would be disappointed.

"I would love to go home."

That was it; I kissed her softly and helped her get off my lap and onto the back of the bike. I revved up the engine, and off we went. She wrapped us in my jacket and held on tight, sliding one hand down the front of my Levi's, over my jeans, making me moan audibly.

"Not fair, Maria. That is Sooooo not fair." My words came out like the moan that I let slip.

She didn't care; she continued to move her hand across the seam of my jeans, making me crazy. The vibration of the cycle, her hand on my jeans, running up and down so slowly and softly; I was losing control. I leaned back on her as we rode the ten miles to my house.

"It's going to be a very long ride..." I said.

At one point, the guy in a car next to us about had an accident, he figured out what she was doing. Maria kindly pointed him out to me, so we could both throw him a smile. Even in my aching, I laughed with her as we watched him lose control, nearly careening of the road.

We finally ended up at my house; it was a whole new ballgame at my house, much freer than anywhere else. Maria turned into a completely different creature, so different than the one I just picked up at the pond. There she was always worried someone from her neighborhood would come up and find us. Here she was more herself.

As we pulled up, her hand moved from my crotch to my breast, teasing me as she giggled and slipped from the bike.

"I can barely walk..." I said as I got off the bike, in great pain. "You are going to pay for this and I mean it." I glared at her in fun. "My jeans are wet and you are proud, aren't you?"

She grinned and moved away from me so I couldn't catch her.

"You are going to pay."

I chased after her. She ran up the walkway to my porch, screened it and opened the door. She ran inside and then pulled the door shut fast and hard.

"You can't keep me out." I said.

"Watch me."

She held onto the screen as hard as she could, using her feet against the doorframe for leverage.

"Oh, please. Do you think that will keep you from me? I would tear strips of wood off the house to get to you, my mi amore. So, give up now?"

I loved when she was playful. She still held fast to the door. I made an effort at opening it, but she had a good grip on it. She laughed at my effort.

"Come on, tough girl." She was being sassy. "All those looks. The dark brown hair, the bluest of blue eyes, those long black, thick eyelashes...yummy. You're feminine curves, those vivacious breasts...Shane, come on, Honey, you can do better than that."

Chapter 2

She was giggling, and it resounded through the porch. Reluctantly, she finally opened the door and let me in.

"There, ya big baby." She said.

I smashed her up against my front door, three steps back; we hit it with force. I kissed her hard and ran my hands up her tank top, through the armhole and under her bra. Tugging at her nipple, I kissed her again.

She spoke against my lips, "I hear a car..."

"Oh, shit. I forgot, I asked Sherry and Mar to come over for dinner and movies tonight.

HONK. HONK...

They were laughing and waving from the car. I yanked my hand out of Maria's shirt to turn and see my friends as they pulled into the drive.

"I can ask them to come back another night?" I was questioning her.

"No. It's okay, really."

"Are you sure?" I looked deep into her eyes. "This is our time together. It's so short."

She nodded and I didn't question her anymore. The girls were getting out of Mar's car and walking up the drive. Maria put herself back together as I stood in front of her while she tired to put her breast back into her bra. I leaned against her hard, preventing her from having room to do it. She was pushing me and I was leaning back even harder, until she laughed.

"Shane." She whined, "Let me get it back in."

Mar and Sherry entered the porch and I eased up so she could finish. I knew I was probably blocking their view, but

I guessed she was embarrassed anyway. She had only me the girls once before when they stopped in one night. We had been making love all night long and the doorbell rang. When I answered it twenty minutes and a hundred rings later, they gave us grief all night.

Sherry was carrying a bag; I knew it was Chinese food. I had completely forgotten we were going to watch movies tonight when Maria called.

"I invited the girls to watch movies tonight." I said to Maria as Mar blew past me, opened the house, knowing it wasn't ever locked, without a word just a big smile on her face.

"Don't mind us, girls." Sherry said, "We know what to do." She kept on walking.

"No shame in either one of them." I shook my head and smiled.

"I am really sorry, Honey, I forgot." I kissed her again before we went into the house.

I figured she would be upset, it infringed upon our time.

"It's okay, meet me in the bathroom in five minutes." She slipped in the house as she said, " Don't dawdle. I'll be waiting for you."

I stood there in awe, no answer, because she had already left and I was standing alone on the porch. I heard her mutter greetings to the girls and excuse herself from the room.

I went inside and sat down with the girls, careful to keep my legs crossed, knowing that Maria had left me wet from the bike.

"So, how are you tonight?" I asked.

They laughed. Sherry, with her usual comeback said, "Not half as good as you. So, she must have called after we talked?"

They knew the whole story, the only ones I had been able to talk to about it. I had told them about Maria only after they caught us the night of the never-ending ringing doorbell. They wouldn't leave that night until I introduced them. They sat there saying, "We know you have someone here, we aren't leaving until you introduce us." And had planted themselves on the couch. Maria had crept down the stairs, shyly, and I had introduced them after coaxing her for twenty minutes that it was okay. I had never regretted telling them. They knew everything of our stolen moments and probably knew that I was a goner.

"Yeah, she called right after." I smiled. "I need to go freshen up. You know where the plates are. Start eating and I will be down shortly."

My five minutes had passed and I was anxiously awaiting my surprise. I had no idea what it was, but I knew it would be well worth the wait. I went up the stairs to my bedroom, but she wasn't in there. I then went to the guest bedroom, again no Maria. I finally saw a light under the door to the restroom and remembered she said to meet her there. I had to be more prepared than I was, so I jetted back to my bedroom and ripped off my shirt, bra and my jeans. Clad only in a black thong, I ran back to the restroom, hoping the girls didn't see me run by the stairway.

I entered slowly. "Oh, my..." I gasped.

Maria was sitting on the edge of the tub in my leather jacket, nothing else, just the jacket. It was open enough that I could see the cleavage I dreamt about each night. She looked at me and started to get up. In the tub the water was running and bubbles were forming.

She had lit candles so I flipped the switch off and let the candles illuminate her lair. Moving my foot forward slowly I began to ascend upon her. As I neared she slid her arms around my waist, laying her head on my stomach. I held her to me, realizing that the amount of feeling I had for her was immense.

"Alone at last." I breathed. I didn't know how much time we had left, but it didn't matter, I would make it count. I moved her shoulders a smidgeon so I could kneel down and meet her; I had to kiss her.

"I missed you so much." She said.

I kissed her softly, holding her face in my hands and restraining every shred of passion I had for her, kissing her ever so gently. Her lips were as soft as rose petal. One time she had sent me roses. She had taken one from the bunch and tore a petal off, placed it on my lips and asked how soft it was. It felt just like her lips.

All of the sudden she pushed me to the floor...off came the jacket...her hands on my breasts...her eyes gleaming. Her hand went from my breasts to hers.

"Oh, Maria..." She wasn't going to...

She made me watch as she did to herself what I wanted so badly to do. How unfair it was to make me watch and when I attempted to touch her, she slapped my hand.

"Not yet..."

The look in her eyes told me to back off. She was straddling me, dripping on me and it was painful in the most wonderful of ways. She was now moaning, very loudly. My thoughts didn't immediately go to the girl's mere rooms away, but rather, my body took over and responded shamelessly. She was moving on me, grinding her hips, while she dabbled.

The floor was cold, the tile beneath me feeling different all the sudden in my excitement. Maria was moaning and I was trying to be quiet so that I could hear her. The floor beckoned to me in some manner. I couldn't close my eyes or I couldn't see her, but I was so close to coming. She was moving so that her hand was pushing against my stomach; she was almost there when I started to scream.

In her delight at my screaming she became furious in her intent. I was trying to move quickly, but every time I tried to get up, she took her other hand from her breast and pushed me back down.

"No...Maria..."

I couldn't get up and the water from the bathtub was tumbling onto the floor. BANG. BANG. The thud of someone's hand on the door was ringing in my ear, as Maria's moaning became so much louder. She was starting to come and her breathing was rapid, her moaning unabashed. I couldn't get her to understand what was going on.

"Hey, you might wanna turn the bathtub off, it's leaking down a vent into the living room." Mar's voice was insistent.

I could hear her and Sherry laughing their asses off outside the door, Maria still working it hard, moaning a little slower, but just as loudly.

Finally Maria figured out what was going on. I was grabbing a towel from my penned-in position and trying to throw it to the edge of the tub to catch some of the water. Maria didn't care. She slid her fingers to my lips, making me taste her. Her other hand went under my thong and slid inside me.

"Oh...shit!!!"

Maria grabbed the towel out of my hand and began mopping up as she worked her magic on me for all of two minutes. I arched my back on the tile, my hair wet from the overflow of the tub.

"It's okay, girls. We have it taken care of. Thanks." Maria was talking to Mar and Sherry.

"Okay. We just wanted you to know. Take your time; we are in no hurry. We'll just start the movie. See ya when you get there." They were laughing hysterically.

All of the sudden Maria took her finger out. I arched more, trying to find them again but they were gone and so was Maria. I felt cold where she had warmed me.

She got up and slid into the tub. She had to almost get in to turn off the water and as she slid in, more water tumbled over the edge. Slyly she looked at me, wanting me to join her. I got up quickly and hit the release button for the water and climbed slowly in, not caring that water, once again, was spilling from the tub ruining my tile floor and probably my venting system. I moved directly on Maria and went to work.

About a half hour later, Maria and I emerged from the bathroom. Clad only in towels with wet hair, we ran to the bedroom. She jumped on the bed, enticing me to make love to her again. She wasn't shy at all with me.

"Come make love to me again, Shane. I miss you so much...
" her passion dripping from her words. "I want you again."

I couldn't pass it up. I went to the side of the bed and grabbed her under the knees with both my arms. Sliding her to the edge of the mattress I immediately began to lick up her leg.

The time she screamed even louder when I touched her with my tongue. I grabbed a pillow, not in time, but stuffed it over her face. She held onto it as she screamed and moaned into it. She began to shake, her body shuddering underneath me as I climbed to kiss her, yanking the pillow away and replacing it with my lips. I held her tightly. I wanted this on a regular basis and yet I knew it would end soon. She always had a time limit. I couldn't help it; I began to cry softly.

We held each other, grabbing each other tightly and holding on while her body still reacted to my former touch. She must have felt my tears on her shoulder, even though I tried to hide them.

Her hand came to my face softly, "Baby, what's wrong?"

I squeezed my eyes shut, trying to stop the tears. I didn't want her to know it hurt sometimes.

"Honey, what's wrong. Please tell me." She was kissing my eyelids.

I just couldn't tell her. I felt a tear drop on my chest. She was above me, kissing my face, stroking my hair. Another dropped on me. She was now crying too.

"What did I do, Shane?" she croaked out softly.

"Nothing, baby, I promise. It's just the emotion. It moved me." I lied.

My hands caressed her, touching her cheek, stroking her lips, assuring her that I was fine. She began to bawl, sobbing out loud. Her head rested rather hard on my shoulder as she became extremely emotional as well. I just held her. It was so hard to do this. We got such intensity between us and when we were together it felt like life was just perfect and without her it wasn't. It was cold like it had been in the bathroom when she was on me and then got up. I didn't know where I stopped and we started when I was with her and without her I didn't feel connected to anything anymore. How could I tell her how hard it was?

Finally she stopped crying and we lay there in each other's arms, our skin touching serenely. I didn't want to move for fear I would hear that she had to go. But, she made no attempt to leave. Usually she would start stirring and have to get up and say it was time to go with this sad little look on her face, but she just stayed in my arms. If I just didn't think about it, maybe it wouldn't happen? I had been so tired this week, all I wanted was for her to stay. I had made plans with the girls, because I didn't want to be alone and think about her and then she had called.

"Honey?" Maria was speaking.

Here it came...she was going to leave. I resigned myself to it with a sigh.

"Honey, are you okay?" she asked.

"Yes. I'm sorry." I smiled at her. I loved looking into her eyes after we made love. She could barely open them; they were heavy and sultry. She looked like she had just made love every time.

"It's okay. You wanna hear the good news?" She moved on top of me so that I could see her. She was breathtaking, I never got used to that.

I nodded. "Sure. I love when you tell me things."

I supposed that she would at least have another hour or so with me and we could have dinner with the girls and watch the movie. I was glad they were here; at least it wouldn't be so bad when I got back from taking her home. Maybe they would ride with me? I wouldn't have to come back to an empty house that smelled like her, her perfume permeated my rooms.

"I'm here for the weekend." She was smiling brilliantly.

"What?" I moved so that I could see her to see if she was joking, that I had heard her right.

"No, really, it's true. I didn't want you to know at first, you are so passionate when we don't have time, like you can't get enough of me and I was selfish. I wanted to have that first." She smiled wickedly. "But, I really do get to stay till Monday morning and then I have to go to class. What do you think?"

I had said nothing. I was speechless. A whole weekend and it was only Wednesday.

"How?" I didn't understand how she could get that much time.

I barely got the word out before her lips were softly

pursuing mine once again. I couldn't think. I kissed her back softly. Wait…I had more than an hour or two…I had almost five days with her.

"I get five days with you?" I smiled. "Are you sure? You aren't teasing me, are you?" Then I got scared. "It won't cause you problems?" I started to ask more questions, but her kisses and her hands running through my hair were driving me crazy.

I heard a moan escape from my lips again. I couldn't ever say no to her. After arousing me again, she stopped. Not that I wanted her to, but she got up from the bed, dramatically pulling herself from me, laughing as she moved, and went to where her clothes were and started pulling on her jeans.

"I lied…" She smiled. "I told my parents that I had a seminar in Oregon that some of the students went to. I gave them your 800-number for the pager. They will never know that I didn't leave town. Shane…I just needed to be with you."

She finished dressing minus her bra and moved to toss me my clothing. She threw them on my face, teasing me. I pulled my jeans on, kicking my feet up in the air, and she pinched my butt. I was laughing, wiggling around trying to get my jeans on and trying to get away from her pinches. Finally, I was dressed. We kissed one last time, longingly, and headed, hand-in-hand, downstairs.

Chapter 3

"Where are you?" I sang out from the bottom of the stairs before turning the corner to where the girls were watching television. They were laughing. We walked to the love seat, where we usually sat together and I pulled Maria in front of me. She leaned her head back against my shoulders.

"Thanks..." Maria said to them. She squeezed my hand as she spoke.

Now they were all laughing.

"Anything to help out." Mar said. "Next time you need to use a bigger pillow or something though." They burst out. Still laughing, barely able to speak, she said, "It was like watching a really bad movie down here." They roared.

Sherry interjected through her laughter, "Yeah, and by the way, your wall over there..." she was pointing, "it's sopping wet from the water leaking through the vents."

I turned beet red. Maria didn't seem to mind as she leaned back and kissed my cheek.

"Maria said she was going to wreck you..." Mar was laughing so hard she was crying. "She just didn't say she was going to wreck your house too."

Their laughter rang through the room. Even Maria was laughing as she high-fived them both.

They were all involved?

"You knew?"

They both nodded as the high-fived each other.

"You rats..."

We finished watching the move; Maria and I picking over

the leftover food and the girls made light of everything with one more laughing rendition and then went home.

Alone again, Maria donned some music. We lit some candles and settled on the floor together. I played with her hair, stroking it softly and twisting it in my fingers as she lay in my lap. She was oddly quiet. It was very sedate; no time frame, no hurry, no scurry to get done what we needed to get done. It was better than a weekend, because we weren't cramming everything into two days.

"Five whole days?"

She nodded. "Heaven."

"Sweetie, want something to drink?" I asked.

"Let me get us a glass of wine." She got up and walked towards the dining room, where the wine cabinet was. "Merlot?"

"Yeah, that's fine."

She poured us each a glass of wine and got some crackers from the cabinet. When she sat back down, she straddled me and fed me the crackers, making me beg for mer. She would hold the crackers at bay, dangling them from her mouth right in front of me, but not let me have any as she sucked it down when I got near. Finally, I threw her on the floor.

I held her arms over her head with one hand and locked her wrists on top of one another so she couldn't move them. She fought to get free so she could continue to tease me, but it didn't work. I held them away and immediately went to her nipples, over the fabric of her shirt and teased them into compliance. I wanted her to be mine. With my other hand, I slid down her legs, over her knees that were bent. She locked her knees on me, not letting me between them. I coaxed her to open her legs as I sucked gently on her nipples. Hearing her moan when I would flick them with my tongue. Finally, after I worked for five minutes or so, she let me between. I teased her for all it was worth, letting go of her arms and moving to her so that I could make love to her. Her was nothing better to show her how much I loved her than this. I could kiss and adore each apart of her body, relentless sin my attempt to cherish her. She entwined her fingers in my hair and arched her back to meet me and then she made love to me, growling as she licked and sucked until I came hard.

My mind never able to hold a thought when she touched me, Maria made me scream. She had a way of coming to me that was unlike anything I had ever experienced. She moved her lips over my body, finding spots I didn't know I had. She would take her time, letting me know how much she appreciated my body and how she made her way over and under every curve was intoxicating.

She played with me, she toyed with me. she drew me to a point of burning passion that made me scream at her…"DON'T stop, Maria…don't stop."

My body flew into it's own world, her at the commands. All night long, we lay on the floor of y living room and paid homage to each other's bodies until we had no energy left.

She swept her hair, wet with perspiration, over to the other side as she said, "Oh, my God…I can't make another move. I can't lift another finger." She spread out on the floor when I finished coming. Dramatically she said, "You have worn me out. And, to think you are so much older." She laughed lightly.

"If I had any energy left, I would make you pay for the older comment, but I don't either. I can't move." I just lay there.

"I have to sleep." She said as she snuggled closer. "I don't even have the energy to get up the stairs. My legs are wet noodles."

"Let's just sleep here." And that is where we fell asleep.

The next morning, I called into work and had my work sent via courier to the house so we could spend the day in. We didn't leave the house much, except to go for a walk in the park. It was an easy stroll with her hand-in-hand, having heads turn when they realized that we were lovers, both women. But, we didn't care. Where I lived, in the neighborhood so far from her own, it was much more relaxed than the devout Catholic area she lived in.

We walked through the autumn leaves, kicking them as we went. She laughed and we played. She picked up a handful of leaves.

"I dare you…" I said, giving her the 'mean' look.

She wasn't scared in the slightest and dumped the leaves on my head. It started a huge fight. She turned and ran and I chased her.

"I will catch you…you little rat." I ran ahead, but she was fast.

"Come on, old lady," she teased over her shoulder twenty feet ahead.

I was intent upon catching her and didn't realize she didn't see the park bench coming up, she was taunting me still with the old lady thing…"Maria…" I yelled. "There's a be…"

She fell into the bench, hit it with her right knee and tumbled over the other side.

"Maria…" I finally got there. "Are you okay?

She was laughing hysterically, tears streaming down her face. She grabbed a pile of leaves from under the bench and threw them in my face, my mouth wide open.

"I'm fine, old lady."

I sputtered and spit. "Ugh…I can't believe you did that."

"Here are some more." She grabbed another pile and tossed them in my shirt as I knelt down to see if she was okay.

There were three boys playing nearby that seemed quite inspired by us our now full-fledged leaf fight. They joined in when Maria tossed leaves at them also. "Here you go boys, drench her with them."

They all began throwing leaves at me, my jacket now covered in dirt and broken leaves and leaves hanging on to strands of my short hair. We threw leaves all over each other, all five of us.

We laughed and we giggled, Maria and I finally teamed up against the boys and chased them till we had them drenched in leaves as well.

"I am having so much fun." I said to her as she tackled one of the boys and dropped leaves in his hood, his mother cheering her on.

"Me too…this is great." She then called to the boys,

"TRUCE! You win. We are too old for this, you are much too good at this game." She was out of breath.

"Awww, c'mon. Just a little more?" One boy said as he tossed some more leaves at her.

"No, sorry. I have to leave. But, I had a great time. Thanks." She hugged each one and told them goodbye.

"Look, there's a vendor. Can we get something to eat?" She said as she grabbed my arm and held my hand, hanging on my sleeve.

The boys followed us and we had hotdogs and listened to their silly jokes as their mother thanked us for playing with them. She didn't seem to mind that we were as close as we were. She even let us buy them an ice cream when we left; they were so disappointed that we had to go.

As we walked back home she said, "Do you dream about things?"

I didn't know what she meant. "Sure I do. Like what?"

"I dream about having a family. Kids and stuff, ya know?" her eyes twinkled. "I want kids."

"I do too. I always have. It's just hard, how are we supposed to have kids as lesbians? I wouldn't mind adopting. I've seen a lot of cases where people have done that, but I want biological kids. I'm too old now." I said slowly.

"I want to be a pediatrician and take care of kids, but I want my own too. How are we going to do it, Shane?" she questioned me but looked away.

We walked a few more feet in silence before she continued, "How are we going to do it, if we want kids, Shane?" she stopped in mid-step and turned to me. She got very close and asked me clearly, "Will we have children?"

"I would like to. There are more adoptive families than there are kids, and it's hard to just go out as lesbians and adopt. It used to be that people said there were a lot of babies out there that needed homes, but at the office we see that isn't actually true. The special needs children, hard to place kids are the ones who need the homes. Maybe we could adopt some of them?"

"I think that would be good. We should stand a good chance of being able to do that as single parents, but not together. We are lucky thought; we can show that either of us is financially s table...well, I will be when I get a job." She smiled at me.

I was hoping that she wasn't just thinking of it as single parents, but that she and I would have a life together. It was the first she had ever really brought it up. I hadn't quite decided if she was serious about being able to handle the life-style.

She leaned forward and kissed me. I knew that she was kissing my soul, because she kissed my forehead, a much deeper emotion than just kissing my lips. I let the conversation go and she didn't bring it up again. She grabbed my hand again and we walked home.

That night we listened to music deep into the night and talked some, mostly made love, enjoying the time together. I got to know a side of her I hadn't seen, different than the sensual or passionate side; a more relaxed, focused and real side of her. She read while I worked and remained attentive to my every need. It was like playing house and I found myself relaxed, continually smiling and content.

The next night we went to a school production at the college. One of her friends was in a play. He had written, directed and produced a one-act play.

"That was amazing." I whispered to her as it ended and everyone began clapping.

She nodded as she clapped and whistled through her fingers. It was about a young gay man on his way out of the closet. It had such depth to it and really told the story well. We had enjoyed it immensely. Afterwards we went to congratulate him.

"Please come to the cast party, Maria. You have to come." He begged her.

She looked at me, "I don't know, Jim..."

I nodded okay; I hadn't been to something like that for years; it might be fun.

"Okay, sure we will." She smiled at him and got directions.

It was great watching kids sit around and discuss the

theatrical end of the production, the missed cues, the mistakes that we hadn't seen. Then the real party started. Maria and I got to dance together for the first time. I forgot sometimes how much younger than I se was, that a few years made a difference. I felt old when we were dancing, watching her groove with the rest of the kids. I was so impressed with the way that she moved. I hadn't been to a club in years and I didn't really feel like I fit in here.

"Dance with me." She coaxed me as I slowed down. She let her eyes rove my body as she moved in front of me, dancing for me.

She wasn't shy about dancing with me, but she made sure a couple of guys were around us at all times, almost dancing with us. Her eyes when they met mine were seductive and passionate. I could tell what she was thinking, and it wasn't about dancing. We danced the night away and had a few too many glasses of wine. I slowed down quite a bit before it was time to leave, but still felt the effects lingering nicely.

After the party, on the way home, I pulled over about two blocks away from the party and put the car in park.

"Do you know how much I love you?" I asked her as I turned to face her in the seat.

She kissed me softly and then pulled me over to her on the seat she was in and slid her hands up my blouse. I kissed her using my lips and tongue to explore the depths of her passion for me. I couldn't move much, but she undid my bra and took advantage of me right there in the car. My legs were stuck on my side, the sports car lacking enough depth for my height. While I was trying to get leverage, Maria pulled the seat incline lever and we flew backwards.

I screamed. "You scared the shit out of me..." as I tore at her with kisses, my hands sliding up her skirt to find no panties.

She laughed at me as she fondled my breasts, kissed my neck and bit my earlobe. Once in a reclined position, we made love. Everything was getting hot and heavy.

"Shit, Maria..." I panted. "My foot is stuck on the dash." I pointed to my foot caught between the steering wheel and the dash near the door.

She pulled to try and get it out and I heard my shirt rip. It caught on her bracelet.

"Your shirt..." She looked horrified. "Your new shirt...I just ripped it." She giggled and then ripped it off my shoulders and tossed it in the back seat. "We don't need that, do we?" Her words were lost in a kiss.

My hands slid over her skin, stopping to make her moan in certain areas. Moving my lips skillfully over her neck, her shoulders and up to her ear, I whispered what I was going to do next. She would moan at the thought before I even got there. Every moan she let slip made me one step closer to exploding, my reactions coming in waves. Somehow her leg had moved over to my seat and in the middle of our escapade she must have put her foot on the horn of the car.

Wrap. Wrap...He banged on the window. "Ladies...roll down the window." The police officer was shining a light in the window.

Maria was half-naked, my blouse was completely off and in the back seat, my bra who knows where...I was between Maria's legs, her legs were over the seat pushing on the steering wheel.

"Oh, shit..." Maria muttered, scrambling to get back in her seat and away from the light of the officer.

I grabbed my blouse from the back seat and put it on, inside out and opened the door. As I practically fell out of the car, the officer laughed and helped me get up by steadying my arm.

I pulled my skirt down and adjusted the blouse the best I could, the buttons were all gone from Maria ripping it off. I then turned to face the officer, completely embarrassed. I hadn't been caught in a situation like this since I was a teenager.

He spoke before I realized who it was. "Well, Miss McAllister, nice to see you."

Shit!!! It was an officer that had just testified against a client I was representing. This was not going to be good.

"Hello, Officer Grant. What can I do for you?" I didn't even try for professionalism.

"Well, since I see its you, there really isn't anything else. I had a complaint from a neighbor that someone was blowing their car horn." He was laughing.

I wasn't too humored until he spoke again. "I think its best I just walk away and let you get back to your friend. By the way, I didn't run the tag yet. I'll just put that some kids were goofing around in the report." He patted me on the back, "I didn't see anything."

I'm glad he thought he was funny. But, I was still in shock. Maria must be sweating bullets, not knowing what was going on. He said goodbye and climbed back in his patrol car and I climbed back in the car.

"What happened?" She asked.

"Well, it seems you had your foot on the car horn." I burst out laughing.

I laughed until tears streamed down my face. It was funny, after all. "I can't believe you didn't know you had your foot on the horn!" I looked at her with tears still in my eyes. "Neither of us even heard it. Isn't that something?"

"That's some serious getting into each other." She said as she laughed with me, her head thrown back.

The whole way home we laughed about the situation. Every time I would look over at her, just after calming down some, I would put my hand on the horn and let it rip. We would bust out in laughter again. It was fun.

The next day, Saturday, we slept in. Not going to bed until four in the morning wasn't something I did all the time. We did nothing but lie in bed and watch movies naked together.

Sunday morning Maria was up at eight and rustled me out of the sheets. She kissed me all over, had made coffee for me and breakfast in bed consisted of bagels, fruit and juice. We ate and lay together.

"What are you wearing to church this morning? We're going to eleven o'clock mass." She grinned shyly, but I knew she was serious.

"You want me to go with you?" I wasn't as stunned as it

sounded when I said it. I thought she would cry, the look on her face.

I had dropped from organized religion in my teens, I prayed very rarely and really didn't know what to make of all of it.

"Well, I thought we could share that. It's very important to me, Shane." She pouted.

I didn't say anything and she got up from the bed and went to the bathroom. After a few moments I followed. I was already naked, so I just climbed in the shower with her. Pinning her against the tile I slid my body next to hers. The water ran down between us and she reached up and smoothed her hair back. It was wet and curly, just like I liked it. I looked her directly in the eye; I wanted to see her reaction.

"I would love to go to church with you, but I'll be real honest…organized religion is condemning and judgmental. I don't think we would be welcome in your church together. How do you feel about that?" I kissed her lips and then went back to searching her eyes for a reaction.

"I refuse to be kicked out of my place of worship because someone has interpreted the Bible to say something that I don't believe it says. I have the Word written on my heart, Shane, and I don't think this is wrong. I know that my family won't understand, but I am free to attend Mass whenever I please, with whomever I please. And…That is that!" she was staunch in her commitment; I had to agree with her.

"Okay, I think I'll wear my black slacks, a white shell and my cardigan sweater, the white one with black and red accents. Does that sound like it'll be okay?" I was teasing her.

I moved my leg between hers and rubbed it against her. She winced a tiny bit.

"Are you okay?"

She nodded. "Yeah, I'm just a little sore, the car wasn't as comfortable as I might have liked," she grinned.

She had to be sore from Friday night- it seemed as though our passion was hard and fast. She had ground her hips into me very hard as she orgasmed. I didn't want to hurt her so I pulled my leg back and placed my hand there, softly and gently. She was still as wet as before. I could feel how hot she was and it made me drip immediately. I couldn't get enough of her, no matter how much I had, I just wanted more. I quickly made love to her, knowing exactly what to do from our experiences together.

The shower was hot against my back and felt good; my aching muscles were tense and raw. My tension increased as I watched her arch her back against the wall, grabbing for the showerhead to hold onto as she moaned my name over and over until she began to shudder against me. I kissed her and held her, rubbing the soap on my hands and washing her gently, never letting go. I held her against me as I washed her and then relaxed as she did the same for me. We then stood in the shower, under the water, soaking it in for what seemed like hours all the while kissing body parts and caressing each other softly with soapy hands.

It was just after ten when we got out of the shower and gathered our things to ready ourselves for church. My clothes were big on her, but she looked great anyway. She had chosen a gray skirt, matching jacket and a white shell that offset her dark eyes and complexion. We pinned the skirt at the waist and she was good to go.

We chose a church close to my house, fearing being seen anywhere near her neighborhood and attended the eleven o'clock services. Before church got started, as we sat in the pew, Maria whispered to me, "Just do what I do." She sort of laughed.

As the music began to play, Maria opened a miselette and began to sing. She had a beautiful voice, something I had not known. I had never heard her sing before. She stood and motioned to me to join her. The priest and his followers walked up the aisle and as the music finished, we sat back down.

This was my first mass, so I wasn't sure what to expect. I had heard that Catholic's did things by far, different than other churches. Throughout Mass there were things we recited, and each time Maria would point out in the book to me with her finger what came next. I kept my place pretty easily. We knelt down and prayed, we sat down, soot up and we sang. I actually enjoyed the music, led by a group of three guitarists. At one point, we began to recite The Lord's Prayer and she grabbed my hand. It scared me until I looked beside me and the elderly lady on my other side was holding her hand out for me to grab it too. She didn't let go right away, like the lady beside me did, but held my hand quite a bit longer.

At communion she stayed sitting with me, while others proceeded down the aisle to accept the Eucharist. In no time the Mass was over and we were heading out the door. We stopped at the priest on the way out, he was in a line at the door, and he hugged Maria and told her it was good to see her. He welcomed us to come again and shook my hand.

In the car Maria leaned back against the headrest and closed her eyes. I thought she must be tired.

Instead she said, "Thank you, Shanie, no one has ever shared that with me before. No friend or boyfriend, no one has ever shared Mass with me. It's something that is so important me, that we share our spirits." She then kissed my cheek, tweaked my nipple and laid her head against my shoulder.

"Do you want to go get something to eat?"

"No," she said, "I would rather go back home with you and just lay on the couch and vegetate." She smiled up at me. "I don't want to be in public. I have to go home tomorrow. It makes me sad. I like this, with you…I like what we have."

Chapter four

That night we ventured out to a restaurant for dinner after remaining in bed most of the day. We actually slept more than we made love and we talked more than we did either of the latter. Carducci's Italian Restaurant was famous for its ambiance. I'd made a call early in the day to secure reservations so that we might dine by nine.

We were enjoying dinner in a corner booth, sitting side-by-side when a woman approached from a neighboring table. I could feel Maria tense immediately. Her hand dropped from mine under the table and she stiffened, moving away from me quickly and roughly.

"Aunt Rosina..." She almost stuttered. "How are you?"

The woman had approached and stopped, a look of disgust on her face.

"Where have you been, Maria? Your mother has been looking for you all weekend." Her hissing made the Spanish more prevalent in her speech, barely understandable. "Monica was in an accident Friday night and they are frantic. You and your seminar," she spit out. "They paged you over and over, finally calling Seattle police and then your school. You weren't even on the trip." The venom seeped out of her speech.

Maria leaned back with her words as if she had been slapped. I had forgotten to turn the pager on. It was at home when I picked her up and I didn't think to turn it on at any time during the weekend. I felt horrible.

Maria was in tears now, "What about Monica? Is she okay? Where is she?"

"They are at the hospital with her still. The scare was

Friday night and Saturday morning. She's going to be fine and the rest of the family is with her...WHERE they SHOULD be. I can drive you there. We just came by here about an hour ago; Uncle Jesse had a client meeting here at the restaurant when I saw you. I am so upset with you. Your lies and your..."

She didn't finish. Maria was getting up from the table.

Rosina continued, "I knew it was you sitting there. Who is she?" She threw a look at me that could have turned me into a pile of ashes.

I shrunk back from the look.

"Are you like 'HIM', tell me you aren't like 'HIM'."

I immediately put together who this woman was. She was the mother of the gay cousin that Maria had told me about, the one who had been excommunicated from the family, namely his mother. This was the woman that Maria kept herself in the closet because of.

Maria turned to me as she got up, cast me a glance that said all I needed to know. It was over. Her family was, by far, more important than I was to her, no matter how much she loved me.

"Can we leave now?" Maria asked Rosina.

It was like I didn't exist, that I wasn't even there anymore and she was going to avoid the question she had been asked. Without hesitation, upon her aunt's nod, she was up and gone from the table, only turning once to look at me on the way out.

I sat there for an hour, until the restaurant closed and they asked me to leave. I was dumbfounded, numb. She was gone, really gone. I didn't really fathom what had just happened. It played back in my mind over and over. I should leave, the waiter filled my water ten times, he handed me my ticket and asked if he could take care of it for me, finally he asked me if I was okay.

"Okay?" I still just sat there.

I couldn't believe this had just happened to me.

I drove home in complete silence; it smelled like her. I

could feel her presence in the car, the warmth she had provided gone, but her presence remaining all the same. I just couldn't ask her what happened or be comforted by her answers. The perfume was worse this time than when she left to go home other times, it was making me sick to my stomach.

At home, I didn't know what to do. I paced the carpet in the living room trying to put on music, but it didn't help; I couldn't even decide what to listen to. My world was upended. I tried the television as a distraction to no avail. Nothing could get the image out of my mind, the look on her face, the rigidity of her body as she left the restaurant. It's all I could think about until I finally cried. I sat on the couch and cried like a baby. I cried for all I had and all I had lost. I cried because I knew it would happen. How stupid could I have been? I knew it was coming and I thought I was prepared. How was I supposed to get to a place that I could really be the saint I was trying to fool myself into being? I cried because I knew that I had fallen in love and now she chose them. They were the bad guys, not me, and, once again, I lost out.

My happiness could never sustain. I could be the lonely ole troll I was before I met her, with women hounding me to go out and my refusing their advances. None of them caught my eye, let alone my interest. I would be a recluse' I couldn't go through this again.

I fell on the couch, laying now and grabbed a cushion, I couldn't find any other comfort and I wailed. I let it loose, let the tears fall. I sobbed at the unfairness and the burden it was placing on my heart. I seethed with anger; life was so unfair. I let my mind wander back to the time when Jay cheated on me. I sobbed even harder and louder. I had broken a promise to myself with Maria and now I was angry about it. I had promised myself that I would never get involved again and I broke that promise.

Jay and I had met six years ago through a mutual friend. Our distance wasn't much of a problem; we transcended the hour easily in the beginning. Somehow we had developed a great friendship, something you didn't get much with lovers in the same respect. She would drive over all the time to see me, surprise me. I fell for her the first time I saw her, when she knocked on my door for the dinner I had invited her to.

She had knocked on the door and I answered, there she was in all her cute ways and she smelled wonderful. I wasn't a big fan of butch women, but she was handsome. I noticed her eyes immediately, even though she wouldn't catch my gaze for long, she was very shy. Her outfit was a big hit as well, dressed very preppy and her cologne was just mesmerizing me throughout the dinner.

It had started out so badly from the beginning, after dating a couple of weeks, almost daily, and her room mate decided that her ex-girlfriend should be informed of her actions and that I was in the picture. It was all over after that. She would go back and forth between the ex and I. I guess I never learned my lesson, because after about six months of worrying about the ex screwing up more of our plans, she seemed to finally disappear. I thought I was in the clear only to find out later about two other women. I hadn't known about them. She had supposedly only slept with the ex once and that was very early on and I had forgiven her, thought it was her 'closure' and gone on. We weren't officially and item, so how could I not?

As I fell asleep on the couch, sobbing through my pain, I remembered how I had moved into Jay's house and made plans with her to have a baby. She had wanted on so badly. Little did I know that it was like a trophy to take back to mom and dad at Christmas? Her words of having children because she loved me were empty and manipulative. When I moved in I wasn't allowed to bring any furniture, to hang pictures, or even bring my own pillows. It was like I was a guest in my own home, very unsettling. Notes, cards, messages on the wipe-away board, you name it...the ex girlfriend was still in that house much more settled than I was. What a fool I had been...I had sold my house and moved that hour just to regret it that badly.

I had cried myself to sleep every night the first two weeks I lived with her. She didn't even notice, or at least pretended not to.

My fitful dreams were of going to the OB-GYN appointments with Jay, having our wills made, how we did everything together. How she looked at me and held my hand. In front of others we were the perfect couple. At home, she never kissed me below my neck, never left my side, just never entered my world. She even charged me rent, all the while; she still had a roommate that had more freedom in the home than I did.

I had gotten on with the firm I now worked with, a Godsend in my wrecked world. By the second month of living with Jay, I found her cheating with someone she had met on the Internet. They had never met, but they had definite plans for that meeting. Jay didn't know it, but I had gotten her Email after reading some notes they had written to each other that she left on the computer.

I finally came to my senses and packed my things and left her. She had left for the weekend away to play with her third woman, one I didn't know about yet and I just packed and moved. I called the realtor and made arrangements in an hour and left. I had been checking into things, due to my overall unhappiness, and utilized one of my options. I knew it was the right thing to do and just couldn't believe I had to do it.

My dreams swiftly switched to the night I moved into my new house. My friends had helped me, quickly and efficiently we had moved everything and I was set up in my new house. I was gone and I was right to go. I had fallen asleep on the couch, not yet comfortable with the living quarters and had a disturbing dream, one that still haunted me at times. I had the same dream as I lay on the couch about Maria.

The long hallway in my house went to the master bedroom. It was really long, and on each side of the hallway the wall texture differed. One side, the southern most, was brick. It had these two white overhangs, for lack of a better phrase. The looked like art belonged on them, they were built with a striking contrast to the brick walls. The north side was all white drywall. Maria and I had walked down that hallway many times. The dream reminded me tat I had a talent to draw, one that I rarely used anymore. I had drawn a lot when I was a child, but rarely, if ever as an adult was I spurred to sketch. In my dream I drew this picture o one of the overhangs of a man. I didn't recognize him clearly, it was like he was a friend to me, something I found utterly fascinating. It brought the hallway to life, a very vivid depiction of this man. After I finished the drawing, in the dream, I stood back to look at it. The man came out of the wall and walked towards me.

I awoke terrified from the dream and lay awake on the couch, my eyes swollen and red. My nose was congested and my head totally stuffed-up. The dream wouldn't leave my mind, my consciousness so I got up to get some wine. I stripped out of my clothing I had worn to the restaurant and hung it over the chair in my room. I then went back down and opened the curio cabinet that held the wet bar. Inside were my charcoals for drawing. I touched them lightly, running my fingers over the paper that covered them.

The dream wouldn't leave me, it followed me like a cloud no matter what room I went into. I didn't care anymore; I had to do something to take my mind off this pain.

"This might just do the trick," I said and grabbed the charcoal and set them on the table. I was now clad in only my panties and bra, in the kitchen I got a couple of bottles of water from the fridge and walked to the stereo. I slid in some CDs, four classical and two Christian that Maria had left. I stacked them in the player and hit random.

With the volume very high, I walked back and got the charcoal and headed for the hallway. I began to draw. For hours I drew out the picture that plagued my mind. Little by little, the drawing began to take life. I remembered so vividly that at one point it made me cry, the emotions coming out. His cheekbones defined as he came to life at my hand I pulled back from my furious line of coal and looked.

He was beautiful. His eyes were much like Maria's probably my interpretation of the comfort he offered me and yet the pain. The tears began to come, he reminded me of Maria as I finished drawing his eyes. They were soft and dark; they held such compassion and care, safety and warmth. His eyes were filled with empathy and insight.

He became my Creator as I continued the evolution. The revelation dawned on me three-quarters of the way through the drawing. It was just at sunrise when it dawned on me that I had drawn Christ Jesus and I recognized him.

I dropped to my knees and knew that the only way I would ever get over Maria was through a power greater than myself. I would lie this down and not take charge, I would find acceptance of something other than what I wanted. The pain I felt was immense, more than I wanted to bear. I didn't know what to do. I had built my dreams in the sand to just watch them wash away. I reached out my weary hand and prayed that He would understand, that He was the only one faithful to me. I hadn't prayed in years.

"Daddy, daddy, do you miss me?" I felt the words slip from my lips. I had been so deceptive in my illusion of religion that I had lost my spirituality. I had been playing hide and seek with my spirit lost in an illusion that I just wasn't good enough to be there. My spirituality had been so great as a child I was always a believer. I couldn't believe that after having laid my life down and finding such comfort in something as a young adult, as a child, that I let someone else convince me that my labor had been for nothing and had moved to be out here on my own in this world. I would rather be here all alone. I wallowed in my seclusion as if I had no hope at all. I had seen it all in motion; pride comes before the fall. I heard the song play in the background as it made sense to me finally and how yesterday Maria had said it and I had not understood.

"Can I be made whole again?" I begged for an answer. "Can I be made free from an offering of my soul at this late point? Can I be made whole again? I couldn't bear you turning from me at this point..." I whispered.

I prayed that if God could hear me that he would teach me to be a better person. I couldn't believe that I had denied him more often than not. It as time to get down on my knees and pray, I knew it. Maria had moved me to find inside me the spirit that once existed, that many years of hearing people tell me I was going to hell made me put a lid on and tuck away somewhere that couldn't be seen, that I couldn't be hurt from it anymore. I had to find it.

I asked for understanding and compassion, for guidance. "How am I going to get through this?" I cried. The music played. JK sang her heart out and it touched me. It moved me to a place that I let out all of the hostilities, that anger rose in me in my profession of truth. "What did I do that was so wrong that you had to punish me like this? In this life, to be punished as if I were a common criminal? What did I do?"

My head was throbbing, my knees hurt, my eyes were swollen and I was so very tired. "The truth shall set you free..." I heard the words.

I got into the shower, left everything as it had been and dressed for work without a care in the world. Not carefree in a good way, but numb from all the pain and tribulation. He had hidden his face from my sins and forgotten everything I had every done and here I had turned my back in Him? I was a horrible person. He could die at Calvary to set me free; to save a wretch like me and this is all the thanks I could give Him?

My day wouldn't stop just because I was in pain. I had things I had to do and by God, I would do them. I learned with Jay that the day didn't stop just because you wanted to lie down and die. It just kept on moving the world didn't let you get off and take a rest. My anger surfaced again for the dastardly things she had done to me, all the lying and cheating and manipulating; how she used me on her arm, because I was 'presentable.' The list was plentiful.

At work I flowed through the emotion, putting in more effort and energy on the cases than needed. They would be the recipients of my pain. At least someone would get something from it. I worked from a sense of anger and it motivated me. I would not let this beat me. Somehow, someway I would find a way out of this and it would be okay. I would find a part of me that I had lost long ago and needed in order to find the serenity that held strong to the fact that His grace is sufficient for me.

Chapter Five

After I got home I looked in the mirror. I hadn't spoken to anyone all day and it was a good thing; no one saw my bloodshot eyes, my swollen eyelids, my hair a mess, because I had done nothing to it after the shower or the lack of sleep that showed in my face. I kept my secret well.

The next few months were a blur of work and Mar and Sherry's attempts to satiate their need to see me do better. I hadn't heard from Maria at all, no contact whatsoever. It had been five months and no word, no letters, no calls...nothing. I had run the full gamut, cried, cursed, gone numb, felt extreme pain; I had hurt intensely. Finally, one night I had been listening to music and a song came on. It had been my breaking point and after that, the sobbing state of muck that I had become changed perception. I had finally asked the pertinent questions and gone to the right place for comfort.

"Why me, Lord? Had I not lost enough? I lost my father, my brother, why this torture?" The words came fast and furious as the final anger at my life's situation unfolded and was discovered. I finally had something to deal with and I did. I even went so far as to question why I couldn't find a good relationship. I had treated women with respect, never cheated, and hadn't even thought about it. Why did I have to be a lesbian? Everyone thought that running to the next relationship was the answer to healing instead of really taking the time to actually heal. It had been the second time I had prayed since Maria left. For some reason I felt unworthy of answers. I kept asking, "Why me, how could you, and why, why, why?" I felt extremely sorry for myself for quite some time.

I didn't really get any answers that night, but for some reason that next day, I felt a hand on my shoulder; in my sorrow, I felt comfort. Where there had been such darkness, I was not afraid. I felt a light shining brightly in my life, the walls had come down and His rays soaked through to warm me, finally…I realized what I was lacking in my life and vowed to myself to get back to me. And, I did. If it had to be without Maria, then so be it, it was for the best.

It had been a few weeks since that 'breakdown,' and I felt a little better. I just worked and kept myself in prayer and reflection on a daily basis. I kept a little motivational journal with me and when I felt the darkness encompass me, I would get it out and find a passage that offered me comfort and somehow the bad passed each time. I finally felt like I had more good in a day than bad and looked forward to getting up in the morning again, if for nothing else than a chance to find something new. A piece of me was beginning to be whole and I had the spirit as my guide, I never had to hide again.

I didn't have to be condemned, because Jesus' death on the cross prevented me from having to do anything. I had salvation by grace and for the first time since I was twelve years old, finding out my sexuality, had felt it. I had grace.

I had peace. I had come with chains that I had gained by fighting wars for my own selfish gains and I had finally accepted his song and my soul felt so empty. It didn't immediately fill with the good intentions and that day in my office I felt that emptiness. How could peace leave such and empty feeling?

My own fears had gotten the best of me for years. Finally they were gone and I was forever looking away from Him. I finally spoke His name and that day when I felt the fire in me for the first time in years, I had to do something about it. I moved to my receptionist.

"Janie, I need the rest of the day off." I turned and walked away.

I knew she would find it nearly impossible to reschedule

my appointments, but I had to do this. I gathered my things quickly and sporadically, not a thing on my mind but going through the motions. I knew what I had to do. Refinement was all I could think of. I had read about it the night before.

I drove until I found the Christian bookstore that I had seen the week before when I was out getting a deposition. There it was. I pulled in and got out of my car. I walked with determination. I had to find something to soothe me. I had a desperate hunger to find His holiness and beauty again. I had to have it. I knew I was in the fire and that my refinement was coming, but it scared me. What did it feel like to be in the fire? Was that what they meant by going through a living hell?

I asked the lady at the counter, "Can you help me please?"

When she looked up, I saw those eyes. Brown and soft, the eyes in my picture on the wall, it was still there. At times, when I couldn't sleep, I would draw on it more. The dream never left me, and now instead of fearing it, I prayed near it with great expectations and anticipation that the Lord would bless me and enlarge my territory. That His hand would be with me, and that He would keep me from causing and feeling such intense pain.

"What can I do for you, Sister?" she spoke so softly.

My eyes began to mist. "I'm stuck." It's all I could get out before the lump in my throat got so big that I couldn't speak. I didn't want to cry in front of her.

"You're very safe here. Let me get you a cup of tea. Would you like to come into the back with me?"

She was the only one working in the small shop, but she took me to the back room after turning a small sign on the door and locking it. "I think you are more important just now." She smiled and touched the small of my back softly and led me to the back room.

It was set up with a couple of chairs and a couch and very warm. She had a little kitchenette and began water to brew the tea.

When she turned back to me she asked, "How long has it been that you are searching?"

I took a deep breath. Her question wasn't intrusive; it was welcome.

"I just don't know where to start." I felt my words on my tongue; I wanted to talk to her. I hadn't gone to a church. I could have gone and spoken to a pastor. I hadn't gone to my mother, an absolute whiz at Scripture. I hadn't gone to my friends for comfort. I had only wanted what He wanted for me, to be in His blessings. I had read the Word as much as I could until I just realized I didn't understand a word of it.

I began slowly, "I turned away long ago and I have been coming back. I just don't know where to come back to."

"Well," she spoke slowly, "I came home a long time ago. Finding home takes a lot of work sometimes and then all at once it seemed to fall into place for me. Why did you come here?" She moved to get the tea as the pot began whistling.

"I saw the store about a week ago and I don't know...I just thought of it today when it seemed that I needed to find something before I could go on. I just know its here, I just have to find it."

"Okay. Fair enough. Can you fill me in on things in your life? I'm not sure what to say to you, but I have been in this position a number of times and what I have always done is to open up my eyes and taken my life beyond it's borders and let God speak to you through me." She turned with the tea. "Can you allow that to happen?"

I thought about it for a moment. It sounded weird. How could she let God speak to me through her?

"I am just a vessel. I try to move beyond my fears and let the love of Christ out to you as if you were my best friend. I know it's strange. But, when I found this store..." She looked to be thinking back in time. "It was twenty-four years ago. Yes, quite some time. When I found this store and the little lady who owned it helped me, I found something I had never known existed. I found peace on earth. Corny as it may sound, it does exist in this fast and furious world. I longed to reach past the world I knew and I had turned away. I had not given credit for anything I did to anyone but me for so long, that I just didn't know if I could do it anymore until I found Helen here at this store."

I let her talk. I didn't know what to expect in coming here and I would do my best to just let it happen and see what came from it.

"Helen sat here, in this very room with me and coaxed me into letting her love me through my pain. You see my baby had just died. She was six months old and died of crib death. I had such intense pain that I didn't want to live. But, I couldn't do that to George." She looked up at me as she sipped on her tea. "George was my husband. He blamed me for her death and I blamed me as well. Anyway," She shook the thought from her head visibly moving. "George divorced me over it. I turned away, and with such a vengeance, I hated. I hated being in this world, but I couldn't do that to George. Somehow through it all, his feelings were more important than mine. So, with my messed up reasoning I stayed alive and in pain until I wandered into this store and met Helen."

She sipped from the tea again. "Why don't you tell me what has happened and I will try to help you." She smiled.

How would I do this? I hadn't really spoken to anyone about it, not even Mar and Sherry. We just 'did' we didn't talk about it. They left me alone and just checked on me occasionally. "I don't really know what to tell you. I'm a lesbian..."

I let the words ring through the room, expecting intense silence. Instead she said, "Does that bother you?"

She asked me that question when I had said it to see if it bothered her. I didn't know what to make of it and while I sat thinking it through, over analyzing like I usually do, she spoke again.

"I don't care what you have done. It's not for me to judge who you are or what you have or have not become. You are here for a reason. We just need to know what it is that you need from being here."

"I've read so much in the Bible in the past five months, but all its done is confuse me. I read about things in the Old Testament that tell me what a rotten lot we are and then I get into the New Testament and I read of this hope, but it still says to not do anything and its made me feel more of a piece of crud than I have ever felt. There is no way that I can be perfect enough to get where I want to be. I just want to love Him. And, I don't feel very worthy of that. I haven't been a very good Christian for quite some time."

"How is it that you are a 'good' Christian?" she asked me.

I thought about it a bit. "I don't know. I guess by doing everything right. I cause people pain. I caused Maria a great amount of pain and I can't get past that. I can't get past the fact that by my being in her life we both have suffered so much."

"Who is Maria?"

"She was my girlfriend, very Catholic and her family didn't like her cousin being homosexual and..." I wasn't doing a very good job explaining and in my frustration tried to spell it out. "I...well, her aunt caught us at a restaurant and she went home with her. I knew that we would one day have to live with a decision she made between her family and us and God and she chose them. I feel like I am being punished. I know how much she loves her family and God even more than that. I didn't know what to do with my anger and in an attempt to resolve it; I started reading. I don't want to be in pain anymore. I just don't know how to explain it..." I was completely frustrated now. "I don't even know your name..." How could I explain my deepest emotions to a complete stranger? "I shouldn't be here." I moved to leave.

"I think you are right where you're supposed to be. Sit back down and give this a chance. And...my name is Mariah."

I didn't know what to do. I was half sitting and half standing and very confused. I looked to her for some sort of answer. Should I stay or should I go and those eyes hit me again, such compassion and understanding. I fell into the chair again with a sigh.

"I just don't know what I need and I don't know where to go to get it."

Mariah said, "You are here, aren't you? Did you just go with what you thought? Didn't you just end up here, in a strangers store and feel when you came in that some sort of answer was here for you?"

I nodded.

"Then let's get to work. I have something, let me get it." She moved from the room and came back moments later with a CD that she put in a player and hit play.

The music drifted through the back room. It was very moving and soft, yet it had passion and it drew from me.

"It's called The Prayer of Jabez." She smiled. "Have you ever heard the prayer?"

I shook my head. I hadn't heard of it.

"Let me show you…" She grabbed her Bible and flipped through the pages. "1st Chronicles 4:9-10. Here is what it says, 'Jabez was more honorable than his brothers. His mother had named him Jabez, saying, 'I gave birth to him in pain.' Jabez cried out to the God of Israel, 'Oh that you would bless me and enlarge my territory! Let your hand be with me, and keep me from harm so that I will be free from pain.' And God granted his request.'"

"That's nice." I said. "That is what I want, no more pain."

"You explained that very prayer while you were talking a few minutes ago. I know you to be right where He wants you at this moment. We all have to have pain. Without pain, we would never know the meaning of pleasure, if that makes sense?"

"Of course it does. I just don't want to hurt THIS bad anymore. I just don't know where to begin to come out of it. My days are better, but it's hard to get through things. I have had some loss in my life and I guess I am just still angry about it. I never was until recently. I just said to myself that it's how it was and that is that and I didn't fully let myself feel. I've been searching through of late to get rid of the resentment and bitterness."

"That's called refinement by fire."

She caught my attention. "I read that last night. I read about the refinement through fire. I just don't get when it stops. How do you know when you're done?" I tried to lighten the situation. "It's getting pretty hot in here."

We both laughed for a minute.

"Yes, it can be quite hot. But, to answer your question, I have a little story that was told to me by Helen, strange enough. When I sat in this very room, she told me of the refinement by fire, what it takes to come out of it with the purification. She told me that there was a group of ladies here in the store for a Bible study and they came upon this verse in Malachi. It told of the refiner sitting and purifying, a purifier of silver. The ladies didn't really get it, so they called a silversmith. They asked him questions like do you have to sit while you refine the silver? He explained that in refining silver, one needed to hold the silver in the middle of the fire where the flames were hottest to burn away all the impurities. He not only had to sit there holding the silver, but he had to keep his eyes on it the whole time it was in the fire. If the silver were left even a moment too long in the flames, it would be destroyed. The women weren't satisfied still. They asked him how do you know when it's done? He said that was an easy one, you know it's done when he could see him image in it."

She sat and let it sink in.

"That's it. That's beautiful. I was reading it and I couldn't make sense of it. It spelled it out and yet, without this knowledge, knowing what you just said, I couldn't get it. If you sit in the fire, number one...you aren't alone, He has to watch you and two...you can't be done until He sees His image in you. That's perfect." I smiled. It finally felt genuine, that the smile was from inside me again.

"I thought that might help you out. It really made sense to me. My unresolved questions really left a hole in me and I couldn't find anything to fill it up. After I felt there was a reason for my pain, it seemed to fit into my life. I found that I could help others by what I learned from my losses and that I was never alone, even without George and my daughter. Somehow it just didn't hurt as much. There was hope."

Chapter Six

I rushed into my office, late for an appointment out at a client's office and tossed my court documents on the desk. I flipped through my messages and grabbed the phone to check my voicemail. The last six weeks, since meeting Mariah had helped a lot. I felt more a whole person. I noticed a difference in my whole demeanor.

There were four voicemail and I jotted down the information as they peeled off their numbers for me to return calls, while I grabbed the documents and file for my meeting. I dropped the pen to the floor as the last message came in. As I reached down to pick it up; I tried to push the number to erase the message I had just listened to and accidentally hit something else and Maria's voice purred in my ear. I lost composure. Her voice went to my very core. I jumped at hearing it and dropped my case, knocked stuff off my desk. For all I had done to get to a good place with me, I felt as if I had failed. I refused to let this bother me; attitude was everything.

"Ugh…I can't be late to this meeting." I said to myself as I looked at my watch; I had ten minutes to get there and it was quite a drive. I began my reflection as to why me…but stopped myself. I knew there was something out there for me; what, I had no idea, but something. I said a quick prayer that Maria was safe and sound and sent my love to her. I then thanked God for His grace and asked for peace in the situation again. Tucking the notes back into my briefcase, I walked out the door, still numb.

In my car, I was deep in thought. The entire drive I was having problems concentrating and even though I pushed

Maria from my mind, she had made her choice. I kept telling myself that. It wasn't helping. I had to meet with Jack St. John, a big client and I hadn't prepared properly. I knew better to go to a meeting unprepared and to be in this frame of mind. I had to reschedule.

I popped my cell out of its holder in the car and dialed. I explained to him that I was unprepared and that we needed to reschedule. He was fine with it and somehow that eased my mind some. In my complete frustration at my attitude, I dialed my mother's number.

"Hello." Her voice was unfamiliar to me. We hadn't really spoken in the last few years and it had been weighing heavily on my heart.

She hated me being a lesbian. I acted as if I had no real family because of it all and she acted as if I didn't exist as well.

"I need help…" I burst into tears. My tears weren't the kind that rolled down your cheeks; these were the alligator tears that stung your nose. I was all involved in the crying, the sobbing when I heard nothing.

"Shane?" she paused. "Shane, is that you?" I had confused her.

I choked out the words, "I need your help."

Mother was very spiritual and maybe she could help. It was hard acting as if my happiness wasn't important, only Maria's. Even in my frustration, my questioning God, I always knew that her happiness was more important to me. Through my sobbing I tried to speak. How she understood me, I hadn't a clue.

"Mom, I don't know what to do. I fell in love and she couldn't be with me, because of her family. I love her so much that I let her go. What do I do? I don't know where to get my answers. I go to God, but it doesn't make it go away. How do you do it? How does someone else matter more than you matter to yourself and it be okay?" I rambled quickly. It fell out of my mouth like the tears fell off my cheeks. The sobbing was bad enough I had to pull the car over. With traffic behind me, I stopped, a complete standstill and cried to my mother.

"You need to leave her alone; her family is more important.

Let her go. You have your career and you need nothing else. You must think of her and of God's wishes for you. You're a strong woman, Shane, and you belong to God. Leave her alone, it was meant to be like that. Her family is what should come first, just like yours..."

She actually made sense to me. For the first time in forever, she made sense. Maria couldn't be without her sisters and brothers, her family was more important. I had to really let her go. All the sudden, I realized that I was talking to my mother. All the pain she had caused me all those years, never being good enough. Her calling me fat, taking me to places so that that I was lucky to have any self-esteem, they were gone; the feelings of animosity towards her were gone. All that anger and frustration, the hate I had for her, it was gone.

"Why don't you come home for a bit, Shane? You can come here and mow my lawn."

"Mom, thanks, but I can't come mow your lawn. I have work to do and I'm going to be okay. Thanks." I hung up the phone and laid my head on my steering wheel. I wasn't sure where to go from here, but I had to go somewhere. I was blocking traffic.

I gathered myself to the best of my ability and conceded that my lot in life was to be alone, to be unhappy in love and to make my family and Maria's family happy, to leave her alone. It didn't matter how I felt, it was she who was important.

It still made me angry. Why was it so hard for me to be happy? It seemed too much to ask, but I gathered that He knew more than I did and would do my best to trust in that. I headed back towards work.

"You know, if you just let me have something to hold onto, I wouldn't be so mad all the time." I laughed at the thought that I was telling God what to do. "I didn't mean it that way." I looked up to the heavens. "I just meant that it's pretty hard and I really do think you want people to be happy or you wouldn't be love." The words I had read, 'God is love,' rescinded through my mind. Love was good; God was good, why couldn't I have some of it?

My cell phone rang. I figured it was probably Mother. I had been curt and she probably was going to bawl me out.

I answered. "Hello."

"Shane, Sherry was in an accident, broke her leg. She's at the hospital. I need help, can you make it there?" Gary was speaking very fast.

I could barely understand him in his hysterics. Fags were such drama queens. Gary was Sherry's roommate and apparently he was with her.

My energy level was so low, but I knew what he was trying to say. Sherry had multiple personality disorder, dissasociative. She hated hospitals and immediately it donned on me that my problems weren't as big as this one.

"I'll be right there, which hospital?"

Sherry had been locked in a psychiatric hospital at the age of twenty for forty-eight days. They wouldn't let her leave and she had just delivered her baby. So, I could just imagine the problems they were having if she slid into one of her alters.

'We're at St. Catherine's on eighty-fifth. Hurry, Shane, no one can deal with her, she's freaking out. She is Rage." He wasn't calming any.

Sherry had an alter she called 'Rage' and Rage wasn't one to reckon with. I had met him only once, after Jay had screwed me over and Rage was going to kill Jay. I had to sweet talk him into not doing anything and he had promised me he wouldn't do anything. After talking to him and resolving that Jay didn't deserve to die, but deserved a slow and painful life here on earth, Rage left and another alter came up. His name befit him, he was all the rage Sherry had stored in her life and when it just got too tough, Rage would come up and could handle things much more efficiently. The years of abuse and suffering that she faced as a child; the molestation and the ritualistic abuse were all stored up in one alter. Rage vented hard.

"Shit. Gary, calm down before I have two crisis on my hands." I tried to calm him some. "I'll be right there, in just minutes. I am in my car now heading that way. Is she bleeding?"

I knew her reaction to blood; she loved it. If she were only bleeding, then I knew that I could help her with Rage present. It was sick in its own right, but it was my only hope. How they would be able to work on her with Rage present, I couldn't see it. Rage was such a bad ass. He was her protector and so pissed off at the world. If he came forward, then it was to protect her or someone she loved. If I could just get her to hear me, I knew I could each her, but Rage hated everyone, me included. The blood would have to be there or I wouldn't be able to help her without them knocking her out and that would make it nearly impossible to gain trust with her ever again.

I sped to the hospital, only minutes away "You do work in strange ways." I said as I laid my foot on the accelerator.

I flew, stealth, into the parking lot and slid my car into a stall at the emergency room entrance and raced inside.

"Sherry Wyck..." I said out of breath.

She pointed to the hallway at the right and I flew that way. I wasn't watching where I was going or I was going too fast; I crashed into someone as I came around the corner, and we both fell to the floor; I was nearly on top of her, her back to me. For a moment my body froze; she looked like Maria from behind. God, not right now, get Maria off my mind. I hadn't time for this inner struggle Sherry needed me.

I was climbing to my feet, adjusting my slacks and slipping my heel back on that had fallen off when I fell, when she spoke.

"Are you okay?" she asked.

I froze in place. It was Maria. She had on scrubs and was in the emergency room.

"What the hell?" She was supposed to be at Oxford, studying with that doctor. That's what I told myself repeatedly that she took the chance she had to make her life. My head was spinning.

Her face lit up. She grabbed me and held me close. I was frigid, stuck, no emotion, no feelings. Why was she here?

"Sherry's here, did you know that?" I said angrily.

I was pissed. What was she doing here? I didn't have time for this. I had just cleared my mind about what was right and what I had to do. What was she doing here? The anger surfaced quickly and hard. And, if she was here, why had she not contacted me? What was going on?

I came back to reality when I saw Sherry come flying out of a room two doors down, limping on her leg. She fell.

We immediately ran to her side.

"Sherry...Sherry, come back up for me, Honey, please come forward." I was nearly screaming at her.

I wanted her to come back so that I could reason with her and didn't have to use the alters. Their personalities were so different from her core. It was hard keeping them straight sometimes.

"Shanie, they won't leave me alone."

That was Becca, her five-year-old personality. There was hope. When distressed, she could slide in and out of alters in a moments notice. I had to work fast.

She began yelling, "MAKE THEM STOP, SHANE. YOU'RE HERE, MAKE THEM STOP."

I replied, "You got it, Rage. I'm gonna make them stop."

Two orderlies came out of the room and tried to grab at her.

I screamed at them, 'Leave her alone. I will take her back in, leave her be."

I did my best to show her that I was on her side. Maria and I helped her up, each with an arm over the shoulder.

"We have to go in there, Becca." I said to her softly, "And look, I found Maria."

She looked at Maria and her eyes lit up. I had struck a cord; she loved Maria, all kids did. I had to convince her that Maria was the reason we were going back into the room. The orderly closest to me decided to be a hero and grabbed for her, pushing Maria out of the way. Big mistake, Buddy.

"GET AWAY FROM ME..." Sherry immediately struck out at the orderly, hitting him square in the head, knocking him against a wall. She fell herself, to one knee. I could see her leg through the torn jeans; it was bleeding. I had to use it; I knew Rage was up again.

"Sher...look, you're bleeding, how cool."

She looked down, distracted momentarily. Her obsession with Rage was apparent; she was a self-mutilator. It had to work.

"Oh, kewl, look at how bad it is." It was like someone else was looking at her leg, that's how it worked, she could disassociate and she didn't feel the pain any longer. She was right with me.

Maria stepped in, "Sherry, can we go in and look at it?"

We grabbed her up again and led her into the room. Maria gave the orderlies looks that definitely said, 'get the hell out of the way.'

We got her back on the table and Maria cut the jeans as she spoke to her, "Sherry, I haven't talked to you in a couple of months, how have you been?" She was working furiously cutting and loosening the material from the swollen and grotesque wound. "I thought about calling you and inviting you to graduation. I graduate next month and I'm going to have a big party over at Shane's. Do you think you could come? And, can you ask Mar for me?"

She had removed the material and continued conversing with her. I saw the orderlies and two doctors coming through the doorway and walked directly to them, hustling them back out the door.

"Who do you think you are?" One asked me.

"I'm a friend of hers, she suffers from multiple personalities. You might need to call in the psych ward, some of them are pretty harsh, but she knows Maria. I know she will freak out of you try and trap her or make her feel like you are doing any medical treatment on her at all. I don't want you to use something to knock her out, because they did that last time and she hid in her house for months. Please work with me?"

They agreed to let Maria handle what she could, but they had to get one of the doctors in there to work with her.

When I returned, I saw Maria talking to her, leaning on one elbow on the table Sherry was laying on discussing graduation. She looked older, classier than before with a maturity of sorts. She looked at me, and when her eyes met mine she looked away quickly. She was supposed to be in England. I had all kinds of questions, mainly massive confusion. I couldn't get her to look at me.

"Shane, why am I here?" Sherry spoke in a meek voice. She must have realized I was back and switched alters again. I knew this one well, Angel. She was a fifteen-year-old girl who was sweet and innocent, not touched by all the bullshit Sherry had been through.

"Hey there, Angel, how are you?" I spoke softly, taking her hand. She wasn't scared like the other alters. She was Sherry's social person she got along with everyone. "I think you had an accident, Darlin. Can you feel any pain? You have a broken leg." I had to test it out. If Angel couldn't feel the pain, they could work without anesthesia or painkillers. I prayed she was the answer we needed. It was freaky how the alters came up to take on roles that needed taken on.

"What do you think, Shane? I don't feel anything. Can they fix it?" She was lost and confused.

Angel could only be here momentarily, Rage could come back at any time. It seemed from studies I had read that the different personalities could actually have different vital statistics and brain wave patterns. The mind was an infamous wonder.

"I think we should let them try, Angel. If I stay with you, can we let them fix it?" I smiled at her and came closer, "That looks pretty bad, I think you could use some medical attention. How about that nice man there? I was just talking to him, he seems very nice and Maria knows him."

"Maria, is it okay?"

"It sure is, Honey. This is my friend, Dr. Jones. Let's see if he can help me."

"I don't like it here, Shane. You have to stay with me. Okay? Promise?"

"Sure, Hon. I'm right here."

I didn't know how much Maria actually knew about Sherry. I had told her a few things, but couldn't remember how much. I looked over at her; she was watching me.

I smiled, "Can you do this?"

She nodded.

Two hours later Sherry's leg was in a cast, they went ahead and put the cat on, because they were afraid that she wouldn't be as cooperative as she was then. She might have to have it redone, but for now, it was set. The blood-curdling scream as the doctor manually set her leg was enough to leave me completely and utterly exhausted, I couldn't imagine how Sherry felt.

Maria had been called out to another room with the doctor she was under; the page had come just as they were finishing up. She had been heading for her lunch break when I slammed into her, that's all I knew.

As she left, she looked at me with those big brown, now sad, eyes, but had walked out the door without saying anything.

Sherry had to stay put for another hour before they got the administrative paperwork done and was dismissed. We talked about all kinds of things, Angel and I. She was still present, so there wasn't a crisis with her disorder. It was nearly ten o'clock at night and I was exhausted. My questions for Maria had gone unanswered.

Mar showed up as we were walking out the door, she couldn't get off work. Sherry was in the wheelchair waiting to be taken out when she walked in.

"Well, look at you two," she said.

We were ready to load Sherry in the car when Mar saw Maria walk to the reception desk. I was standing with my back to Maria, but when I saw the look on Mar's face I knew she had seen her. Her jaw was open and her eyes were fixed.

Quietly, almost in a whisper, she said, "Shane...Maria. Maria's in the waiting area."

I hadn't had time to tell her what had happened.

"I know, Hon, she helped us with Sherry; it's a long story. I don't know what to do, we didn't talk at all." I turned to look at her; she was standing with her back to us. I looked at Mar, wanting her to tell me what to do.

"Go talk to her, Shane. You can't leave without knowing something. You've been wrecked over this for too long. I want to know too. Why is she here?" She must have just thought about England too, we had discussed how it would be so much easier and that being in England left no way for me to contact her. "I thought she had..." She trailed off as Maria turned around to find us watching her.

Maria started walking toward us, out the doors. I stiffened and grabbed Mar's hand, Sherry safely inside the car. She neared, looking directly at me, but turned when she got close enough.

"Hi, Mar. Nice to see you. Can I borrow Shane for a moment?" She turned to me, "can we go for coffee? I was just looking for you, hoping I hadn't missed you. I owe you an explanation." She looked the same as before, my Maria.

Mar squeezed my hand.

"Of course you can." Mar said looking at me.

"Yeah. I'd like that." I said.

Mar moved to give me a hug and whispered in my ear, "My phone is on, call me if you need me, but get your answers. You know we love you. It's going to be okay, you did the right thing."

I knew that Mar and Sherry had been through this knowing how I felt about Maria. And that said so much. I had really gone into such a depression after that night in the restaurant. She had walked right out of my life.

"You take care, Maria." Mar said walking around the car to get in.

I used to dial her pager number and then hang up; it wasn't worth ruining her life. I had known from the beginning that Maria was not comfortable with the lifestyle, but somewhere inside me, I wanted to know that she really loved me and that the time we spent wasn't something I made up in my mind. I wanted answers. I could let her go, if it was the right thing to do, but I wanted to fight for her to hold her and coddle her and to give her happiness. I wanted that family she spoke of, that we shared. At least my friends didn't push me. They let me go at my own speed, putting this in the right place. Now I was confronted and I knew nothing but that I needed answers.

Mar stopped, door wide open and walked back around the car to Maria. "I mean that, Maria, take care of yourself," she said as pulled Maria close in a hug.

Maria closed her eyes and hugged Mar back.

"I will, Mar, I sure will."

The hug ended and Mar moved back to the car and got in, the girls swept off leaving me along with Maria.

We said nothing for more than five minutes; just stood there looking at each other. I didn't know what to say; it was very uncomfortable.

"Can we take your car, Shane? I still don't drive." She said finally.

I snapped back into reality and answered, "sure."

I motioned to where I parked and let her go first, unlocking the door for her, as always. She slid in and I moved to my side and we headed off.

❧

"There's a coffee shop up the street a couple of blocks," she pointed, "unless you would rather go up into the country to Sam's..." she hesitated, "I would rather take a drive, if you don't mind?"

I wasn't sure exactly what was going on; sometimes we used to take drives and would stop at this little café called Sam's. We had coffee and very fattening breakfasts, whatever time we were there. I realized I was starving.

"Sam's would be fine."

She reached for the CD pack and put two CDs in the changer then she sat back in the seat and closed her eyes.

I was trying to use my peripheral vision to look at her; I was really confused. I would remain silent and see what happened. There was such power in silence. We drove quite awhile in that silence to the point it was terribly frustrating for me. The music drowned out the engine, she has picked some jazz, rough and passionate.

I pulled up to a stop sign to turn onto the highway; Sam's was just a couple of miles up the road when Maria's hand touched mine.

"Shane?"

I turned to look at her as her lips pressed against mine. She had moved so quickly that it caught me off guard. She kissed me very softly, her hands moving to my head, pulling me more fully to her lips.

I didn't know how to respond. I had so many questions. I couldn't let my heart rule this one; it had to be my head. I didn't respond to her and I turned to just pull her into a hug and held her there.

I felt her start to cry softly.

"It's okay, Maria. I just have to know what happened before I go any farther with this." I comforted her, felt her pain and felt that she had actually missed me too. Emotions rushed in, I was back five months ago, flooding my world, my senses racing with excitement. Damn it!!! I couldn't let my body control this; it had to be a thought out process, safety for me; it had to be right. There were five months of my life for her to account for, five months of intense pain and thought-provoking worry.

"What happened that night, Maria?" I whispered as I kissed her head.

She moved so she could lay her head against y shoulder, more relaxed as I hugged her. Her hand was sitting lightly on my leg, caressing, and the other hand in my hair, softly stroking it as I spoke.

"I left the restaurant that night and went to the hospital. Monica was fine. She'd been banged around a big, but from what she said, it wasn't that bad. The family flew into hysterics and made a huge deal over it, because she had snuck out with her boyfriend. That was the biggest part of it. My family hates him and they had been drinking. So, when he lost control of the vehicle and crashed into the ditch, Monica got to put all the blame on him and not on her sneaking out. She hit the dash, but other than a bump on her head, she was fine." She moved a little to get more comfortable. "Aunt Rosina was in a tizzy. She'd made the whole thing such a big ordeal and when she saw me in the restaurant she freaked. Mama just wanted me to know that Monica had been in the accident; When Rosina couldn't page me, they started to worry and called the school. That's when they found I wasn't on the trip. They didn't know what to think, because I had never lied to them before, so it was something huge." She moved to face me. "I'm sorry, Shane."

I nodded; my answers weren't complete by far.

"When Rosina saw us together, it gave her ammo, the ammo she had been looking for. She immediately went to the lesbian thing. I think she knew right off; she probably had been watching us from her table. I felt so bad, Shane. I lied to my family."

She was speaking softly still, stroking my hair and holding me close to her, laying again now on my shoulder.

"They didn't deserve that, Shane. No one deserved me lying. I should be okay with my lifestyle, if it's right. Apparently it isn't right. Aunt Rosina and I talked in the car. I freaked on her, right there I yelled at her and told her I didn't care if they kicked me out of the family, if she had me exorcised...I didn't care what she did to me. All I cared about was you and the kids. She had cried and then apologized to me. She told me that every day she wished that she had a chance to tell Jaime that she was sorry, that she was his mother and she loved him. Uncle Jesse sat there until Aunt Rosina told me that I could never see you again; through her tears she said I couldn't see you anymore, because it wasn't right." She held my face in her hands now. "Shane I only cared about you."

I had no idea what to say. If she cared about only me, then why didn't she contact me? She didn't even call me or tell me what was going on? It didn't make sense, but she had never lied to me. While I was thinking about this, she cradled my face. I kissed her hand lightly and closed my eyes and tried to listen to her.

"Uncle Jesse freaked out. He told Rosina straight up that she had just done it again. She had just tried to ruin someone else's life. He said he hadn't seen his son since the day she found out he was gay and he wasn't about to let her decide someone else's life, to make someone else lost what he lost, his son. He told her that she had caused Jaime to leave and that Jaime had died alone and afraid. Jesse said he would never forgive himself for not taking a stance and being there for his son, whom he loved very much. I couldn't believe he stood up to her for the first time that I had ever seen. And, he told her that he wasn't going to sit by and let her do this again, ruling the family as if she were its judge and juror. After that, he turned to me and asked me if I thought I was sinning. I told him no; that it was the only thing that felt right to me and that I had waited twenty-five years to find you. I had not had love in twenty-five years and had known since I was very young that I was different." She looked deep into my eyes and held my gaze.

"Uncle Jesse asked me something. He promised that our conversation would go no farther than the three of us. All he asked was if I could do him a favor. I said I would try and he asked if I could go six months without seeing you, a period consistent with what he thought was long enough to see if you still loved me or if you were like a lot of other gay people, that you just wanted sexual fix...so to speak." She watched me for a reaction and got none. "I promised him I would do it. I knew you would be waiting for me and that there wouldn't be anyone else. He told me if I could do that for him, he would make certain my Aunt had no chance to ruin my life with you and that he would welcome us into their home as a family from that point forward." She laughed a little, "Aunt Rosina tried to butt in and he put her in her place immediately."

"He did?"

"He sure did. I love it. He also said to me that I better read up on what the Bible said on premarital sex and make sure that I was doing my best to keep that in the right context."

She moved in her seat so that she was sitting on her legs, her feet curled up under her in the seat; she moved close to me and kissed me softly. "I am abiding by that; I wanted to know also that you would wait for me, because I want to spend the rest of my life with you, Shane. I want you to be a part of my family and I had faith that you would be there for me when I came back. Tonight threw a glitch in my plans though. I couldn't see you and blow you off and not tell you what happened, when it was so close to the time I could come back. I only have two and a half more weeks left, Shane. Uncle Jesse promised me, Shane. I got his word and it gives us the best of both worlds, you and my family. I can do this. I am only here telling you this now, because I love you, baby." She kissed me softly. "I love you so much; we can do this...right?"

I smiled inside from head to toe. She had proven with grand faith, that I loved her and that she could come back and get me and take me home. I would be a part of her family and she mine.

"I can do this, Maria, without a doubt, I can do this. I just didn't understand and it hurt so much. Why didn't you call me?"

"I promised NO contact, none. If I would have called, you could have just counted down the days, but like this you had to really feel it. If you wouldn't have, you would have been out with someone else and done things..." She trailed off.

Fright filled her eyes.

"No, Sweetie, there isn't anyone else." I stopped, "Well, yes there is. There is someone new in my life."

Her face melted.

"I met God again. It took me going very deep inside myself to let you go. I kept telling myself that if I really loved you I would let you go and have your family, because they were more important. God, I tried so hard to let you go."

"You couldn't, could you?"

I shook my head, "No, you are so much a part of me." I kissed her and held her not wanting to let go. The scent of her hair filtered softly into my sense. "I can do this; I have been so lonely, missing you..."

"I missed you too, Shane." She was smiling again. Her eyes

lit up, "I have to keep my word to the best of my ability, so I can't stay long tonight. I want to be sure this is what we both want and I did promise Jesse. I promised I wouldn't contact you and I would deny you that contact had you tried to contact me. It was so hard, but you do understand, don't you? No matter how many times I almost dialed your number, I never called. I even thought about calling you at the office, just so I could hear your voice, but I did not cheat. I would have only been cheating myself. After praying about this in chapel while you finished up with Sherry tonight, I felt it would be okay to explain to you at this point. I thought that if I didn't explain, you would never be willing to let me back in and I have worried about that so much anyway that I had to do it. I know I hurt you, but when we are done, I can give you a whole person and not a shell that has to lie about who she is. It's important to me that you understand my value system and my religion along with this."

It made perfect sense to me. I understood what she was doing and for all the time I put in missing her, I would actually get a lifetime out of it.

"Maria..."

She buried her head in my shoulder and held on tightly. I had so yearned for this closeness, the feeling of warmth I got from her. There would be no more partial nights, stolen phone calls, moments in heated exchange, unless we wanted them. That was enough to take it to the point I could pledge my life to her and I knew that.

"Maria...it's okay, let's do what we have to do. And, I assure you there has been and will never be anyone else for me. I love you. You are the keeper of my heart. I cherish you and always will."

Chapter Seven

The next two weeks were spent in extremely high spirits. My work was more organized and my caseload for some reason was lighter. I finished the case with Jack, settled out of court for quite a bit more than we thought we would get and everyone was walking lighter. Sherry didn't have to have another cast put on after the swelling went down and things were back to normal, for me, anyway. I let the time pass with no worry. I was looking forward to having my life back again, the pain of the last five months almost forgotten.

I even went a step further. At night I would read on the Internet about Catholicism, researching her religion. It was intriguing and I decided that I would like to convert to Maria's religion so that we could share a more thorough spiritual existence with each other. I found quite a bit of information; so much so that it flooded me, so I called Maria's church and made an appointment with a priest.

My appointment with Father Shrader was something that made me nervous. Being a believer growing up didn't help with understanding what being a Catholic meant. I'd heard people cut down and criticize Catholicism, but when Father explained away my questions, it made perfect sense. I saw what Maria saw in it; it's vast and rich tradition. He offered enrollment in a class and I attended before I spoke to Maria again.

Maria and I had made plans for dinner at Jesse and Rosina's on the very day that ended our six months. I had one weekend before we were to attend that Tuesday. We still couldn't see each other or converse in any way until dinner that night and I didn't yet know what her aunt and uncle thought about it, but she promised she would make it happen and I was just supposed to be there at seven o'clock.

I spent the weekend tanning, shopping, walking in the park, and thinking about how I wanted to do it, proposing to her. Maybe a holy union would be just the thing for us. My shopping sprees were filled with gifts purchased for her in my excitement to pass the time until I could see her. I even knew there was a chance she would say no to the holy union, but its something I wanted.

Monday was uneventful at work, so around noon I called Sherry and Mar and asked them for dinner; I was getting restless. Mar agreed she would go by and pick up Sherry and meet me at eight o'clock. Janie took care of most of my load and I was out of the office by six so I stopped by the restaurant and grabbed some Italian food and blazed home.

They showed up right on time and we discussed my plans over dinner. Most of it was news to them; they hadn't pressed the issue, but had called a hundred times to check on me. I guess my not saying anything led them to believe things didn't work out. This surprised them quite a bit.

"So, she did it all for you?" Mar said, "That's amazing, completely shitty, but amazing."

"I know. I thought so too, at first. But, then I tried to put myself in her position. Remember, I'm her first. She will never stop loving me, even if we don't make it, I'm her first love and we all remember our first loves forever. I still remember mine, Angela. She has a special place and always will. Do you remember your firsts?" I asked.

"Hail yes," Sherry said, "She was Puerto Rican and mean." She laughed, "But I loved her and that was that. I put up with anything she did and it was all okay. I think we give a hundred percent to our first loves, because we haven't yet learned how to guard ourselves. Ya know?"

Mar agreed. "I only got a kiss from my first love. She was a teacher of mine. And, it was so horrible. I had such a crush on her." She laughed. "I remember being all google-eyed at her most of the time and she would blow me off. One day after school, I was maybe fifteen, I just laid a kiss on her and she totally freaked out. She told me how horrible I was and how it was a shame that I wasn't a couple of years older and that she wasn't with someone. I will never forget that."

"You're kidding?" I said. "I thought you were straight until a lot later."

"I was. I just forgot about her. It didn't go anywhere. I decided that I was just displacing my emotions and...well, whatever. I just never told anyone."

We all laughed. Once dinner was finished the girls left, wishing me luck with the following night and I felt like it was going to be okay.

I fell asleep reading and my dreams that night were of Maria, of holding her and finding her a new home. Why a new home? I awoke in a state of grogginess. I had a hard time shaking the dream; it had disturbed me. It was only five o'clock and I couldn't get back to sleep, so I decided to go in early to work.

My day was very full and it ran by rather quickly. At about three o'clock I got a call from Maria.

"Shane. Hi, Sweetie. I wanted to check and make sure that you were coming tonight. Everything is set up."

"I wouldn't miss it for anything."

"My mom and dad are coming too...we are coming out tonight, Shane, to everyone." She sounded worried. Her voice was quiet and demure, very nervous. "I'm afraid, Shane. What if it goes badly? I won't be able t do this. I can't lose my family." She was in tears. "Can I meet you before we go over? Can I come to your house?" she was pleading with me when she didn't need to.

"Maria, why wouldn't you be able to come over, you are welcome anytime, anywhere that I am you are welcome, Sweetie. What time were you thinking about?" my mind flew to my planner. I thrust it open and checked my appointments. I had been careful not to schedule anything too late, because I knew of the dinner. "I could actually leave now, if you want me to, Maria."

"As soon as you can get there. What time is it now?" She sounded a bit more relaxed.

"I'll leave in about ten minutes. Wanna meet me there or do you want me to pick you up?" I figured she was at school or the hospital. It was going to be hard, no wonder she was stressing, with her parents coming along too. I would definitely be the bad guy here. "Are you sure about this, Maria? Your family is so important to you. Are you sure?"

"Pick me up, I'm at the student center across from the hospital. I'm sure, I just have to see you before." She hung up.

I pulled up and she walked to the car, a vision of loveliness. She opened the door and knelt on the seat as she moved across to hug me. She kissed me fully on the lips and held me tight.

"I missed you so much. So much you will never know how bad it hurt to not see you, Shane." She said.

I didn't care who saw, I took her face in my hands, smiled at her and then kissed her again, hard and passionately. "It's over...it's finally over. I'm so glad it's over."

"I know. It's finally all about us now."

She moved back so that she could sit in the seat and I wanted to rip off the skin-tight black shirt and the white shirt that showed so much cleavage that I could taste it. She tossed her jacket over the seat and sat down. Her hair was piled sloppily on her head and somehow made her even more attractive. Her beauty astounded me each time I saw her, but it had been so long since I had really gotten to visualize her without a crisis that today took my breath away.

"Quit looking at me like that." She said.

"Like what?"

"Like you could devour me at any moment," she said, her silky smile baiting me.

"Quit smiling at me like that or I WILL devour you."

She grabbed my hand and we rode in silence the short ride home.

I had only been in love once before, my first love and it

had taken me so long to get over her that I had a string of bad relationships after. Maria was a part of me and without her it felt as though something was missing.

I asked her, "Can you make me a promise?"

"I can try. What do you want?"

I studied her for a moment, "Promise that we won't ever go through something like this again where we don't talk."

"I couldn't take it if we did. I promise. Even if it doesn't work out, let's still be friends." She kissed me softly. "I wrote you every day."

"You did?"

"Yes. I wrote to you everyday, and at night I would pray that you knew I was thinking about you. After awhile, when it was so hard and, I admit, I had some doubts, I wrote on the same sheets two and three nights on one." She got in her bag as and pulled out a big stack of envelopes that were bound by a rubber band. "I kept them for you."

She laid the letters across my lap and as she pulled her hand away, it slid across my leg and my body jumped; she could barely touch me and my body reacted to her.

"I want you to read them sometime while I lay in your lap. Or, I could read them to you. Okay?" She seemed to be a little insecure about us lately.

I wondered if this had taken its toll on her too? She was younger and she worked harder, maybe she had enough distraction to keep her free of pain. I needed to be the mature one.

"That sounds nice." I pulled into the drive and we went into the house.

Once inside she said, "Shane...it can't be like it was before."

"I Know. I heard what you said, do you need a hug?"

She fell into my arms. It was almost four o'clock. We had to be to dinner at seven. I didn't know why she had asked me to pick her up, sometimes before she would clam up when she had things on her mind. I didn't know whether to broach anything or just remain silent and let her do her thing. I just held her.

She sighed heavily, "I don't know what will happen tonight. I changed my whole life so that I could please my family, find myself and create a career. Now it all depends on one night's events. How am I supposed to feel?"

She wasn't any more ready for tonight than I was. I lingered in thought the last few days about just what it would be like with her aunt and uncle and now there were her parents to contend with as well. I had wondered just how rude and lascivious her family could be, my images almost grotesque at times. I understood how it all relied on one night's affair.

"I wish we didn't have to go," I said. It was true; I didn't want to chance more of her running away from me and it hit me that it was a possibility.

"I know, me too."

I became almost angry, "It seems like we are proving something to them that we already know shouldn't be taken for granted. I don't understand why we necessarily have to prove that we are okay being gay. But, I know life well enough to know that they don't understand, very few people do. I have always gone on the assumption, Maria that if they don't like me for who I am, fuck 'em. But, I also gave up on my family, my friends that were straight, and to some degree most religions because they didn't understand. I let people with shallow minds decide where I was allowed to go and whom I was to be seen with. I didn't even know that I was playing the game until you and I met. I then realized how much being in the closet wasn't really different than what I did. I am really cautious about who knows about me, because of my profession. Who wants a 'dyke' for an attorney? They want me, because I am a good attorney, or they don't. It doesn't have anything to do with my sexuality. Now that I see how much I hide it, it befuddles me to think of the kind of righteous bullshit I slung when I was younger. I was one of those dykes that said, 'hey...see me, I am me, and you can't change me.' But, in reality, I hid it from people that mattered to me. I was willing to say look at me, only if you didn't matter to me and I had nothing to lose. I really didn't get into the real me until just recently. While you were gone, Maria, I got back to the real essence of me."

I took a deep breath and kissed her head, "I guess what I am trying to say is that you and I will be together for us, not for anyone else. We have to do what is right inside us. I prayed about it and found my answer is getting back to the real me. I find myself to be in a really bad spot with you, when I stand in front of my Lord, I find that our sexual behavior was inappropriate. We were really out of bounds with it. All I could see is how much I craved you physically and until you were gone, that was a big part of our relationship. I missed more than that though. The Lord showed me that I missed your mind, your comfort, your compassion, your zest and your life for life. I missed the aspects of you that I shared in my life. Everything seemed brighter when I shared it with you. It had nothing to do with me making love to you." I dropped my head, I was failing miserably trying to explain this to her.

"Shane, do you mean this?" She leaned back to look into my eyes.

"Yes..."

"I just want my life, Shane. I don't want loving you to mean that I can't have my family, my friends, my work...I love you with all my heart; I've known that since a week after I left the restaurant, before that I thought I knew, but I KNEW it then. I found myself pushing the thought of you out of my head. I could push out the sexual part, even though I could still feel you against my body when I lie down for the night; I could feel you next to me sitting in a chair or wherever I was. I knew that what I really missed the most was your voice; the way you made me feel. I had called Aunt Rosina and asked to speak to her more. I tried to explain to her that every time I made love to you that I prayed for forgiveness. I hated being this way, a lesbian. All my life I looked for someone to love like my friends loved. I felt cheated. All the men and boy that I saw, nothing in them touched me like you did. I even tried going against my urges and slept with men; I felt so disgusting afterwards." She shuddered. "The day I saw you in the library, something in me clicked.

I couldn't take my eyes off of you standing there, your little glasses coming off your nose, really in deep thought. And, when you turned and saw me watching you, I had no shame. I didn't feel like I had anything to hide; I felt whole. Now they try and make me feel dirty and ashamed. I felt dirty and ashamed with men. I don't feel that way with you; I feel beautiful and whole, complete in me. The church says that I can love you, they give me credit for being born this way...or at least not being able to change it, but they ask me not to touch you. How can I not show you that I love you? When...I do."

"I know, Maria. I've been doing my research on the church." I led her to the couch. She knew nothing of my church activity. "Can I get you something to drink before we sit down? I'm getting a bottled water."

She nodded no.

When I came back from the kitchen I brought the dozen red roses and six white that I had gotten for her. I arranged them like I wanted them and they were ready. I would just give them to her early so she could enjoy them. I returned with them hidden behind my back.

"I have something for you..." I smiled. "I wanted to show you that I love you in different ways, to take a more sensual approach than before. We were so physical" I sighed, "I guess it's inappropriate, because we aren't married yet. I want to be in harmony with you spiritually, emotionally, physically and mentally. It's important for me to know that we are on the same level and that we can share equally. Even when we are in different places; I would like to be able to share everything with you."

I knelt down beside her, the flowers still behind my back. Positioning herself on the couch, she lay in waiting. I had no expectations in this, yet I had the highest of expectations. Immediately a bolt of fear shot through my body; my mind raced, what if it didn't turn out like I planned? What if she needed more time? What if...

"Shane, are you okay?"

My lunch welled in my stomach and a hot flash flew through my body.

"You're so pale all of the sudden, are you okay?" She reached up and touched my forehead. "You're sweating. What's wrong?"

I leaned forward and kissed her, my lips softly sliding across hers, moving and groping for some sort of assurance from her that this is what she wanted. She pulled my body closer, the couch prohibiting us from touching. I couldn't get my mind to stop running its course of negativity even as she kissed me. I pulled back.

I slowly brought the flowers from behind my back, keeping my eyes from hers.

"They're beautiful." She kissed me quickly as she touched the flowers, bringing them to her nose to smell them. She closed her eyes and inhaled. "Mmmmmm..."

"You like them?" I wanted to say my piece before she opened the card, so when she reached for it, I grabbed her hand. "Not just yet...I want to become Catholic." I let the words slip out, not knowing her reaction I searched her eyes intently.

She looked up abruptly. Her brows furrowed in disbelief.

"Yeah...I want to convert to Catholicism, to share with you. I started a class on it...I have a question for you, it's really important to me, well, to us." I stammered.

My hands started to sweat; I could feel the sweat run down my back even though it wasn't that warm in the house.

"Read the card." I instructed her. I took one of her hands, making it difficult to get the card, so I helped her with my free hand.

She began reading the card I had placed in the flowers the night before after my Catechism class. It said: Maria, you are the light in my day, he awareness in my lift. Because of you I am a better person. I am more willing to look at the truth in my life; more willing to be honest with myself; more likely to look at you from the inside out to see the beauty that enhances my life. Because I have known what life is without you, I have a question..."

She looked to me as she finished reading and I took the ring that was tied to one of the flower stems she had overlooked and untied it as she watched. I pulled the ribbon and the ring slipped into my hand.

Her eyes were bright and the tears were welling. Not spilling over, the tears sat where the light bouncing off them enhanced the beauty of her eyes.

I took a deep breath, willing the lump in my throat to go down enough to speak, "I would like you to be my life partner, sharing our lives together, whatever that may bring. And, I would like to make that known in front of our family and friends, in front of God. Will you be my life partner?"

I watched her smile fade and the tears spill. My heart sunk. Big alligator tears grew and dropped to her cheeks, rolling down her face and spilling on her skirt as her head dropped. I had gone too far; she wasn't ready. I could kick myself in the head. What a fool. I blew it...

The tears stung my eyes...and then I felt her hands on my face, lifting it to her. Her lips tore at mine her passion rising, peaking and then falling as she softly finished the kiss drawing her lips from mine ever so slowly. She moved to the floor, sliding gracefully off the couch and molding her body next to mine in an embrace.

"I would love to." She held out her hand so that I could slip the ring on her finger. Looking at it and then to me and then to the ring, she kissed it and then placed her lips lovingly on mine.

Chapter Eight

"Talk about walking into the fire." Maria said as we pulled up to Rosina and Jesse's.

"No kidding. I am sweating. I don't think the shower helped me one bit." I smiled weakly. My nerves were getting the best of me.

We were about twenty minutes early, because we wanted to talk to Jesse before we had to confront anyone. We had spent the last couple of hours contemplating the rest of our lives and had decided that Maria would attend classes with me for the conversion as often as she could. We were going to ask if we could take pre-marital classes offered to the community, knowing it was a long shot, but at least we could ask. And, we had decided that we would then take our holy union to a non-denominational minister to perform so that we didn't offend the church in any way.

We wanted to at least try and have our families treat our relationship as they did a straight relationship. We had commitment far beyond the sexual issues and would try and show them that. We also wanted to pledge to them that we would remain celibate, even though we had already been intimate. We wanted to know that our relationship had the best chance to see the vows through till the end.

We entered the house and sat with Uncle Jesse and Maria attempted to explain this all to him.

"You two have had time together, haven't you?" he still appeared calm, " I am ready to fight to the death, to come out of my shell and fight the fight to the death to have acceptance in the family even if it comes to a resolution that your relationship needs to be kept from those that can't handle it."

We were confused. Maria said, "I don't understand...I thought you would be upset?"

"Not at all." His thick Spanish accent drifted in and out of his speech. "I know that losing Jaime would allow me to show them the response to losing you. They aren't losing anything, Maria; they are gaining a family member. If you need help, I am here for you. Worst case would be that the rest of the family denies you and your relationship, because I can't speak for anyone but me, but I am here for you. You are like a daughter to me anyway, you will always be one of my children."

"Thank you, Uncle Jesse," Maria stood and hugged him. "I am so afraid. Are you sure we need to tell them?"

He pushed her to arms length, his hands on her upper arms, "Yes, I am sure of it. I would have liked Jaime to have been able to talk to us."

Even I could see the sadness reflected in his eyes momentarily, before he shook it off and said, "They aren't going to take it well, we all know that, but..." he smiled, "we are taking them with a surprise attack and that will be to our advantage."

He laughed and it was easier to at least breathe for a minute. Rosina entered the room. I hadn't realized how much she and Maria resembled each other. The night in the restaurant her demeanor was so staunch and the look on her face so ugly that it didn't reveal the softness she now had.

"Shane? It is Shane, right?" she spoke directly to me.

"Yes, Ma'am, Shane McAllister." I sounded stupid.

We laughed. Maria put her hand on mine as it hung to my side; I had gotten up when Rosina had addressed me to shake her hand. I extended it to her.

"Well, Miss McAllister, you look very nice tonight. I like your outfit. Would you like to help me in the kitchen? Maria said you were a pretty good cook." She warmly invited me.

"I would like that. Yes, Ma'am." At least I wouldn't have to be there when Maria's parents rang. This was going to be harder than I had even thought. No matter how supportive they were, Maria's parents could totally freak out. The plan was to have dinner and let them get to know me as Rosina and Jesse's guest and then over coffee Maria and Uncle Jesse would 'break the news' to them. It was a crapshoot from there. At least they would have a chance to like me for me or not before they knew.

I moved off to the kitchen with Rosina and helped with the rest of the meal. The house was very "Spanish" and quiet "Catholic." It was filled with statues of Mary, of crosses and Biblical representation. There wasn't really anything to do and so Rosina took me on a tour of the house.

"I just wanted you to be able to relax without sitting in there like you were in the fire pit. Let me show you the house, it'll give us something to do." She smiled softly at me, a huge difference from the night at the restaurant.

The house was nice, very homey and Rosina asked a lot of questions about my political aspirations, did I have any? And, she talked a lot about my career.

"I had aspirations of being an attorney when I was young. We didn't have the money for me to go to college and then I met Jesse. So," She shrugged, "I will just have to ask you questions." She smiled.

"I don't mind. I like talking about it."

"I am a business man's wife. I just take a very large role in making his decisions. I probably control him." She grinned.

She was very intelligent and spoke of community events she had attended, asking me if I had been. She talked of her children and how Maria fit in with their family.

"She is like a daughter to us. We get a little over protective. So...do you have plans for political movement? Does your sexuality prevent that?"

"Well, I haven't really been in a position to take a leap yet. I don't think it would really matter, my sexuality, but I am just not cut out for it. I support my candidates and take a back role in that way."

I heard the knock at the door. The flame rose from my feet, the fear electrifying, it rose from my feet, through my legs, left a sour feeling in my stomach, tensed my shoulders and ended at the top of my head with my ears bright red.

"Don't worry, Shane. Deidre will listen to what Jesse says. It won't come quickly, but at least you have a chance. Maria said that sneaking around was too hard on her. Give it some time." She patted my arm, much shorter than I.

I was terrified. This is what it meant to be in the fire and for some reason the story of the silversmith and the refinement came to mind. I hoped that He would see His image in me soon. It was surely too hot for me to be comfortable.

I smoothed my dress, swallowed hard and said, "Thank you. I'll give it my best shot."

"Just be yourself, Shane, that's all we can ask for and it will do just fine."

❧

I had worn a simple dress, elegant, yet feminine and not too way out there. I'd worn in to court a couple of times when I needed the jury to see me with the respect of a true woman. Maria's parents wouldn't know right off that I was her lover; this really was an ambush. I knew two things; one, it wasn't going to go well no matter what and two, Maria would not give them up for me. Tonight would determine how she made decisions about us and all the dreaming this afternoon could fly out the door, if they didn't at least say that they would try. With a huge sigh, I moved behind Rosina to the living room.

Dinner was tense, but nice. Jesse had introduced me to Maria's parents, Albert and Deidre, as Rosina's friend. I had been politely shocked when she introduced me and caught Maria's quick glance and knew that she was as well. She seemed pale through the entire dinner, sitting across the table next to her father with her mother seated next to me. She barely ate a thing, pushing her food around on her plate and not contributing much to the conversation. A few times through dinner I reached my foot under the table and tapped her foot so that she would know that I was there. Each time I got a small smile.

After dinner I helped Rosina clear the dishes and prepare coffee for everyone.

"It's going quite well…don't you think?"

"Yeah." Was all I could get out.

"I wondered if they suspected anything when Albert addressed her that one time and she couldn't hardly say anything. I feel for that poor girl, for both of you this evening."

"You covered for her nicely." Rosina had steered the conversation from her right back to business where it had been and pretty much remained the rest of the dinner.

She put the coffee on a serving tray and stopped to look at me, "It's time," she said. "You keep the faith. My baby died because of my actions and I get this one chance to make it up to him. Jaime will be smiling on us tonight and if there is a way…" tears brimmed her lashes, "then he will help us out. Not another family member will have to face what he did." She looked at me with such pain, "Not if I can help it. Jesse and I will do what we can." She took a deep breath; the tears disappeared somehow.

Maria had told me that she had talked to Rosina and that she had explained to Maria that the night in the restaurant Rosina had such hate for me. She had never seen Maria happier after having watched us for quite some time that night. She feared that someone else was taking one of her beloved into that lifestyle and she had immense hatred for it. Rosina had said, "You two were talking and laughing and sitting so closely holding hands under the table. I had to go back and forgive myself for killing my son. I never realized that Jesse hated me for it." She hadn't known that until the night after they dropped Maria off at the hospital to see Monica that he had hated her. She had gone back and searched until she found that she was the one that erred. Jaime couldn't help being the way he was and that they missed out on the time with him before he died. That Jesse hated her for not letting them and hated himself for not having stood up to them. They had renewed faith in their relationship because of it and for that and for the chance to make amends they were going to help us.

I was just about to say something and Maria walked in.

"Shane, I can't do this. I can't do this, Rosina. I just can't…
"

She was extremely pale, her color almost gone to a greenish hue.

"You look terrible. Are you okay?" I asked.

"I can't do this. Mama is in there talking about Christmas and the family and how Monica is finally coming around. I can't do this." Her eyes pleaded with me to get her out of there. I was afraid to touch her, for fear her parents would walk in.

"Take her upstairs and I will come up in a few minutes. Get her a cold rag and take some food up for her. You have to eat something Maria." She handed me a bowl of fruit salad that she had prepared to put in the fridge.

"C'mon, let's go. It's almost over, Maria. Can you make the stairs? You look horrible." She had only been sick around me once, when she had the cramps and puked all night and that is exactly how she looked right now, maybe even worse.

"I feel sick, Shane…" She ran up the stairs and into the bathroom, barely making it before she was throwing up.

I got a cloth, wet it and placed it on her forehead. Pushing her hair up and twisting it in a knot I held it while she was sick, her stomach retching so hard it took her knees off the floor with each convulsion.

"Oh, Baby…" I tried to console her.

I couldn't make her lose her family. THIS is how much this all meant to her and for the first time I realized exactly what I had done to her by coming into her life.

"We don't have to do this, Maria. It doesn't have to happen, we can go back to like it was. There is no reason to tear yourself up like this. You don't have to give anything up for me. I can't do that to you. I won't. I can't." I felt like crying and fleeing so that she could have back her serenity and her peace. She finished heaving and lay back in my arms.

"Shane?" She whispered hoarsely.

I wiped her forehead and her face gently with the cold cloth, brushing her hair back to the side. "Yes, Sweetie?"

"I have to do this. If I don't then I am lying to them and I

can't lie to them. I'll be fine, I just didn't eat anything today."
She took my hands and wrapped them around her from behind
as she scooted into my lap fully. "I just don't want them to
hate me. I can't give you up again. They won't understand that
though...will they?" I felt her tears drop onto my arm.

I kissed her head over and over in reassurance. "It'll be
okay, it has to be..." My words were interrupted.

"Oh, really?" Deidre's voice behind me startled me. " You
KNOW what will happen, do you?"

Maria jumped ten feet, scrambled to her feet and was
visibly wobbling, holding the sink basin to steady herself as she
faced her mother. Her face looked as if she had been physically
slapped. My heart went to her; we were so screwed. I just sat
there.

Deidre spoke again, "You don't know anything, Maria."
Her voice had softened immensely. She reached out a hand to
help me up as she moved past me to Maria.

I was flabbergasted. She wasn't freaking. She moved to
Maria and held out her arms to her.

"C'mere." Maria fell into her arms sobbing as if a dam had
broken, sobbing audibly as she lay in her mother's arms. Deidre
held her and rocked softly as she stroked her hair. "You should
have known me better than this, Nina. Do you think I haven't
known this about you? I knew when you mourned Jaime's
death as you did. I never thought you had problems with it,
just that you never brought it into my house. I figured you had
something when you started sneaking off last year. Why didn't
you just tell me? You used to tell me everything?" She kissed her
head. "Don't you remember that?"

Maria said nothing for quite some time, regaining control
and the sobs residing.

"I didn't know, Mama. I thought you would do what
Rosina did and I couldn't bare that. I tried Mama; I tried to
leave Shane. I put us through hell. I hate it without her..." She
reached for my hand.

It felt weird to hold her hand, even if her mother couldn't
see it.

"I've prayed for you for years, Maria. I didn't know how to ask you about it, but I knew you weren't happy with men. When you had spoken those times about how you and your boyfriend, Reynaldo...remember him? How you two got along, something was not right. You kept explaining how you were so happy with him, but your eyes did not light up. Just now, I stood outside the room and listened to her help you."

She didn't say my name.

"I heard her talk to you and saw how she held you and what she did." She hesitated, never looking at me.

"I talked to Father and he says that you were probably born this way. I don't know if it's right or wrong. He said the church believes and acknowledges it, but that the sex is wrong. Only you know what to do, Maria. I can't say I support you in something that will put you through what it will, but I am the one who told you long ago to follow your heart."

Maria nodded through her tears, still softly crying.

"Your father knows nothing and I won't have it any other way."

Rosina came in behind us. "Is everything okay?"

"Zina," Deidre said in a curt voice, "You are lucky that Albert went to the bathroom when he did and I figured out what was going on. You laid in waiting for us and I won't have that brought on him like that."

"We just wanted to help out so that we didn't have someone make a mistake like I did, Deidre." Rosina was soft yet firm.

"I would have been offended to have been snuck up on like this." She backed away from Maria and stood where she could see us all, four of us in that tiny bathroom.

She spoke again, "I don't know what Albert's views are, he is a man of very few words, but I won't have him snuck up on, it's not your place to tell him something like this in front of others, definitely not in front of Shane. I want you to do this on your own some day, Maria. He is devout and might not take it very well. I have to say; I don't agree with it, I have a very hard time with it. And, from the looks of it, with you sick over it, you don't either."

Deidre addressed me, standing directly in front of me she said, "Nice to finally meet you, Shane. I really used to wonder what you were like that you could take her away from us so easily." Her bit. "She isn't very good at sneaking out, I didn't know where she was going, but I knew."

Maria and I stood there until Deidre walked from the room with Rosina.

"Oh my God, she scared the shit out of me." I said, still afraid to touch her.

"All of this was un-necessary?" She tried to laugh, but the pain still registered. Her color had come back and her features had softened again. She was Daddy's girl and hopefully that would be enough that Albert would be okay with things. She walked the two steps to me deliberately, slowly, eyeing me as she moved her face to within inches of mine, teasing. Just as I closed my eyes to kiss her, she grabbed my breast playfully and laughed.

When we got back downstairs Deidre was putting on her coat and Albert was saying goodbye to Jesse.

Albert came to me and said, "Shane, it was nice to meet you. I've never met a lady attorney." They departed.

After they left, Jesse laughed, "Well, that didn't go as planned. What happened upstairs?"

He went to the liquor cabinet and poured us all a Brandy. He handed us the snifters and said to Maria, "I thought we were going to lose you there, you were as white as a ghost." He teased.

"It wasn't easy. It made me sick. I kept thinking that she was going to yell at me and that Daddy would just walk out the door and leave me behind...forever."

"Well, that's not what happened." Rosina said.

"No, it's not. And, in all of this, I know one thing. I am exhausted and it's time to go home." With that, we made our way home saying our goodbyes.

We climbed in the car and I asked Maria, "Do you want me to take you home now?"

"Can I come home with you?"

We headed home. I had to wake her up when we got there; she was so tired she fell asleep in the car.

We headed straight for the bedroom and before I knew what was happening she had my dress unzipped, clear down the back. I was all over that, grabbing her and kissing as I removed her skirt and undid the buttons on her shirt. She kissed my shoulder, sliding my dress off of it slowly and all the way down my arm, as slowly as she slid the dress down, she kissed her way down my body, finally letting it drop to the floor.

I was standing in my bra, t-back and a pair of sandals. She then kissed down my neck, stopping at the hollow of my nape to run her tongue across my collarbone. I moaned softly. She kissed down my chest to the clasp of my bra, a front fastener and snapped it open, her eyes fixed on mine. She didn't touch them; she kissed between them and blew her hot breath over my nipples, making them stand at attention. She kissed down my stomach, sliding her hands over y sides and resting them just above my hipbones and then dropped gracefully to her knees and kissed my stomach all over, pulling my hips to her.

I knew I was dripping wet, but it didn't matter; I also knew she didn't want to make love to me; we had decided to wait. She was exploring. Her index finger slid under the waistband of my panties at my hip and she pulled them slowly down my legs, kissing the whole time down to my calves. The road back up was as much fun and then she stood in front of me, possibly suggesting it was my turn?

I raised a brow. Could I do this? In my own naked awareness I wasn't sure I could trust myself to go past her gleaming desire and not touch. I quickly asked for strength and then touched her softly.

My hands cradled her face as I kissed her softly, resting my lips on hers and then licking quickly. I forced her lips apart with mine and kissed her like I had been wanting to for two days, weakening even my own knees. I moved my hand down to her jacket and unbuttoned it slowly, smearing her lipstick with the sultry kiss. I couldn't go as slowly as she did.

"I want you naked."

How could I refrain from making love to her? How could she do this and make it look so easy? I never had a reason to stop before. With lesbians it wasn't that I was promiscuous, but it wasn't like we had a reason to not make love. I kicked off my shoes and reached down her legs, one at a time, to do the same for her. She was now standing in her bra and panties, standing, waiting for me.

I laid her back on the bed and excused myself. "I'll be right back."

Down the stairs I went, naked, to the kitchen and grabbed cheese, crackers, strawberries, kiwi, pineapple pieces, bananas, ice, bottled water and two wine glasses. Then to the wine cabinet for a bottle of wine and back up the stairs I bound. She was right where I left her, on the bed. But, she wasn't waiting for me; she was sound asleep. I sat down lightly; trying not to disturb her, she slept so peacefully. Stroking her hair while she slept I whispered how much I loved her...and lay beside her quietly.

The phone rang a half hour later.

I reached for it quickly, upset that it woke her up. "Hello." I was rather abrupt.

She snuggled into me closer, not quite waking up all the way. It was Mar. I told her quietly what had happened and how it turned out and that things would be fine. After we hung up Maria stirred again.

"Is she okay?" she asked.

"Who? Mar?" I didn't know she was awake. "Yes, she just wanted to know how things went. She's fine."

"Mmmm...okay. Where did you go?"

"I ran downstairs to get some food for you and some wine. You were asleep when I got back, so I just sat here with you."

"I'm not tired anymore. Will you talk to me, just so I can hear your voice?"

"Not tired...huh?" I stood up quickly and grabbed her legs

playfully, pulling her around the bed so that I could lie between her legs, but first, I ripped her panties down her legs and held them up dramatically. Dropping them on the floor, over the side of the bed; I moved like a panther, crawling over her. I stopped at her bra and slid my hand underneath her back and popped the latch. With my teeth, I pulled it off, showing off just a little.

"Ahhhh, naked at last." She said as she grabbed some cheese and crackers off the plate I had brought up and began nibbling, paying me no never-mind.

He body was as beautiful as ever. While she nibbled on the good, I lay beside her, running my finger up and down her body, everywhere I could reach.

"You intoxicate me, Maria. I missed you so much. I can't believe how much it hurt. I thought I was doing the right thing letting you go, but it hurt like hail. I started praying."

I waited for her to react. She didn't.

"I even got some answers." Again I waited.

"Keep talking, I want to hear your voice...keep telling me about it." She leaned so she could see me, moving the plate with her so she could keep eating. "I have my appetite back." She explained with a little smile.

"Well, I came to the realization that God was profound in my life, that He was my source of strength. There was no way I could get over missing you; I couldn't have made it through a single day without Him. I missed that, thinking that being gay I couldn't partake of His love anymore. I was wrong."

She licked her finger, "Shane, God would never not think you are worthy of His love. His love is unconditional; He loves you no matter what. Your job, so to speak, is to live by His commands for His will and to love Him more than anything else and to love your neighbor as you love yourself. To do these things, you will be doing what He wants you to do." She was so matter-of-fact.

"Then why all the big to-do about being gay?" I was confused. "Doesn't the Bible say being gay is wrong?"

"Well, there are some passages that state that a man should not lie with a man and a woman with a woman. Also, it says that sexual immorality is against God's will, but it isn't specific. I have researched it some and found it to be very much so a gray area. I don't know what to make of it. I do know that IN Hebrews it talks about a second covenant with the house of Israel and Judah. He says that He put His laws in their minds and writes them on their hearts. He alone will be our God and we will be His people. No longer will a man teach his neighbor or a man his brother and have them say 'know the Lord,' because we will all know Him. And, it says He will forgive our wickedness and remember our sins no more..." She moved a bit, "It gives me courage to search my soul."

Soaking in all she said, to the best of my ability, I still was confused. "So, what does that really mean? Are you okay with being with me?"

She yawned, "I found the parts of the Bible that said that wasn't God's will for a man to lie with a man and a woman with a woman. But, I also found where the new covenant says we have the answers inside of us and given the opportunity to evaluate self, I find that I am okay with it. I go before God in all my nakedness and vulnerability and ask Him. That is what matters, what He thinks."

"What does He say to you when you go before Him?"

"Yes. That it's okay and that He doesn't condemn us for something so intrinsic. I have spent so much time wondering if it was okay and if I were going to lose His love for loving you. I stand before Him and ask, 'why me? Why did you make me this way?' And, from what I understand I am okay and He knew long before I did what was and is going to happen. What mystifies me is that the moment we get Biblical with someone, a discussion or condemnation, I revert back to judgment placed up on me and start feeling guilty, second guessing myself and I lose my peace with it. I get so confused."

I soaked in what she was saying, almost afraid to give my opinion; I knew so little. Her wisdom was so profound and in comparison I was so uneducated, literally and practically.

"I don't get why we are so condemned then. I haven't really found anything in the Bible that they suggest is our final blow.

No clear passages say that. And does it actually state the word, 'homosexuality'?"

"No, there is a biggg..." She yawned again and tried talking through it, "debate over that. The translation could be that it meant men having orgies in the temple. But, there is no 'good' word for the translation. I, myself, can see that having orgies in the temple, gay or straight, would be bad. Promiscuous sex isn't appropriate in my world. I think what I am trying to say," She yawned yet again. "Oh...I am sooo tired. I'm saying that what is right for me is right for me and I have it written deep within to know the difference between right and wrong."

"Sweetie, we can talk about this another time." She was so tired.

"I don't want to miss out on my time with you. I miss you so much. I don't know how long you will let me stay." She smiled.

"How long do you want to stay? We made our pact, no sex!!!" I teased.

We hadn't discussed anything past this evening. Maybe she was afraid to go home?

"I'm more comfortable than I've ever been about my family, that's why I want to stay here with you. I took a week off. I told them I had to attend to some family matters and it won't hurt me at all. They said I could make up my work. I don't have to go back until next Monday." She kissed me.

This time a real kiss, a Maria kiss, pushing her body into mine and pulling anything she could out of me with it. Crushing me to her, she laid her skin next to mine everywhere that she could, touching every part of her that was accessible. Love pounded in every fiber of the exchange, a more compelling notion to find me inside the touching of our bodies, to revel in the attention and the commitment that freely flowed for the first time. Our hands remained intact, never roving or arousing, but rather an exploration of emotion that I had never felt before. It was fulfilling and satiating, absorbing all the emotion that was there.

After a few hours of sleep we woke to each other in a completely different light. I had to go to work, so it was not a typical morning for me. I hadn't planned anything out, so my appointments started early and ran late.

"You won't be home until when?" Maria asked.

"Not till after eight. I didn't think you would be here, so I kept things business as usual and I can't change these. Are you sure you want to stay here? I won't be disappointed if you don't, or maybe you could come back when I get off?" we weren't certain exactly how to handle our new arrangement and with so little time to plan it was a mess. I ran around trying to get my hair done, while she chased me from room to room, trying to get me to get naked again.

"Just flash me those beautiful breast and I will leave you alone." She pled.

"Maria," I laughed and flashed her for the tenth time. "Now, let me get ready." My gray pinstriped suit was tidy.

"Why don't you let me fix up the house? Now, that's an idea..." She mused. "That's it. Can I? Can I? Let me do some things around the house. That'll keep me busy while you are gone."

"I don't care. Do whatever you want to." I said as I put the finishing touches on my hair and make-up in the mirror. "Do you want my credit card? You can order whatever you want and put it on there. Don't spend a mint, I do have a limit, you know."

"I will call you at work and okay things before I do it. I can surprise you. I have always wanted to do something like this. You know...out back, can I build a deck?"

I laughed at the thought of her out back building anything. "I honestly don't care if I come home and you have every room painted and the whole likes of it different. Just don't mess with the drawing in the hallway."

"I noticed that last night. You have some explaining to do..."

"I am sure I do and tonight I will tell you all about it. Now, I have to get out the door. Thanks for making the coffee for me." I said as I ran out the door with bags and coffee in tow. "I love you, Maria."

She kissed me goodbye at the door in just a pair of boxers. She had done more than just flash me as I tried to get my shower taken, not allowing her entrance in or I would have not been able to uphold the no sex rule.

"I love you too. Wait to be surprised. I have a lot of work to do." She smiled.

⌘

I got home from work that night after four phone calls from Maria telling me the amounts of money she was putting on the credit card. I had written them down and the total was near $2,100. I cringed at the thought of what $2,100 would do to my house. What in the world was she doing?

When I pulled up I found two other cars in the drive and had to park on the street. I didn't recognize either one. Upon entry into the house I smelled something wonderful and heard a ruckus out back. I went through the kitchen and opened the oven to find cheese enchiladas baking and rice and beans on the stove. Out back, I found five women pounding away on what looked to be a new deck.

"Holy night! What in the world?"

"I didn't hear you pull up, Sugar." She hugged me quickly and turned to spread her arms. "What do you think?"

"I think you look great in a tool belt." I whispered as the other girls stopped doing what they were doing and came over.

Maria introduced us. "This is Elaine, Randi, Amy and Kim."

They shook my hand one at a time. They looked like lesbians, but I wasn't sure.

"The girls came over to help me out. I met them at a meeting that I went to a couple of months ago, a Christian lesbian meeting. I have friends now." She smiled broadly, clad in a pair of boxers, a t-shirt, white socks rolled down over work boots and a tool belt.

I walked out to where I could get a good look. The deck

had a frame and the whole floor had been laid "You work fast." I said as I turned to Kim, she seemed to be in charge.

"We told Maria it would take a couple of days, but she was adamant about only being available through Friday, but I think we can get it done. I have class tomorrow, but other than that I think we can get it all done. What'da think?"

"Oh, I am no expert on building anything. I dial a phone and have someone else do the fun stuff. It looks great…"

Maria tossed in, "I learned how to attach ledger board." Beaming at her success.

"I bet you did, Baby."

Kim said, "She had no idea what she was doing, but we got a plan and I think we can make it work."

"I need to run and grab dinner out of the oven, Sweetie. I'll be right back. You girls want a glass of wine or a beer?"

They all tossed their drink orders and ten minutes later Maria came back out with drinks and dinner and the table settings for the lawn furniture. She proceeded to spread it all out and I excused myself to change.

Upstairs after I changed, I glanced out the window to find the girls laughing and playing. Maria was dishing out dinner for everyone and laughing and having a good time. I had never seen her with girls her own age. And, lesbians even? What had she been up to that I didn't know about? Was I jealous? I watched out the window and it didn't bother me at all; it was good to see her settling into some sort of life. I hadn't any interaction with anyone but my colleagues, clients and Sherry and Mar for so long that new friends might be fun. I headed back downstairs.

Maria caught me coming out the door and whistled. "Nice outfit…"

Everyone cracked up laughing.

"What? I am ready to help out." I had put on a holy pair of jeans, half the rear-end was ripped out and a wife-beater tank top. My boots were old, but ready for the task at hand. "Should I go change?"

Randi tossed out, "It's a far cry from that suit." And, once again they all giggled.

"Are y'all picking on me?" I said as I sat down next to Maria to a plate that she had filled for me.

We ate and laughed, they were quite fun and afterwards the girls all left and Maria and I sat outside as the sun went down. It was getting chilly.

"Are you cold?" She asked as she snuggled up in my chair with me.

"Not really, as long as you sit with me I'm fine." I said then asked, "Where did you meet the girls again?"

"I told you that I did a lot of things while we were apart. I started going to this Christian lesbian group that I found a flyer to at school. It's a group that was started at the school for girls who had conflict in their spirituality. I really like it. We have a Bible study and they have meetings every other week. I met Kim and Randi there and they already knew Elaine and Amy. Kim and I have become pretty close friends. She is Catholic as well, even thought about being a nun. She and Randi have been together for almost four years and Elaine and Amy have been a couple for six months. They met right before I found the group and started coming about the same time that I did." She turned to face me as best she could. "It's okay, isn't it?"

"Of course it is, Silly. It's just that in some ways you are so different. I mean, I never really knew you in a social sense, it was always just the two of us except the few times that Mar and Sherry was over. Until last night, we never really did anything other than just the two of us. I guess we have a lot to learn about each other."

"It's a good thing, because I sin in my mind all the time. I can't stop thinking about making love to you. Do you realize that last night was the first time that we were together that we didn't make love?"

"Was it?" I faked ignorance, very well aware and knowing just how hard it was going to be to continue in this manner.

"What will we do when it's too hard?" she asked.

"I don't know. I thought about that at work today. I don't have any good ideas. I guess you could just go home or I could go to Mar's."

"I decided that we needed a project at all times. If we have something else to do, for our betterment, of course, we could at least adjourn to it. I took three cold showers this morning and all that made me do was take care of myself and fantasize about you." She smiled a wicked grin. "I don't think that's any better than actually making love. I would have been in the shower all day had it not been for the deck." She looked over at her project.

They had finished anchoring it to the house, had the post holes dug, filled with cement and the base set. It wouldn't take long before they had it finished.

"That might last for about three days at this rate. And, I might add, it looks great. Is it two story?"

"Uh huh," she nodded. "It will have stairs on that side and rails on the top. I think I can do the rails by myself, but I could hardly lift one of the beams that went into the ground. Randi and Kim did most of the lifting and the rest of us just did what they said. I like wearing the tool belt...made me feel butch." She flexed her arm muscle.

Laughing I said, "Well, what else do you have planned? And, what is it I am supposed to do? I don't have time to take cold showers and you know I don't like playing by myself. I can't believe you are comfortable with it."

We had talked once about the fact that I didn't like to 'play with myself' as I called it, too embarrassed to even say the word. Maria thought it a healthy exploration of ones body and a way to achieve a sense of self in a relationship, a way of knowing what felt good and what didn't.

"I know you don't, Honey, so we will have to figure something else out, won't we?"

"Like what? What else can I do? Last night lying with you was fine. I know that I don't have to make love to you, but watching you from the upstairs window a while ago, just sitting and laughing with the girls, I could have devoured you in seconds. How am I going to control the desire? I know it's not going to go away."

"I don't know. I guess the only suggestion I have is to take it one step at a time and wear really ugly clothes that cover every part of your body, unlike the nice tank you have on right now." She reached around and grabbed my breast and got up and ran into the house laughing.

I chased her inside. "Where did you go?" I yelled not finding her in the kitchen.

"Come and find me."

I heard her in the next room but when I got there she was gone.

"Oh...Mariaaaa...where are you?"

"In herrrrrrre." Sounded from a couple of rooms over, my den perhaps.

In my den there was nothing. I wandered through the den to the utility room, to the spare bedroom downstairs and finally the bath. Nothing. I climbed the stairs listening for any movement. Nothing. I turned at the top of the stairs and moving away from my bedroom checked the spare bedroom, my office, the library, the bathroom and only had two rooms left.

"Maria...where are you now?"

She said nothing.

"Maria...whereeee are you?"

"Right here, where I have been for fifteen minutes waiting for you." She said from the room opposite my bedroom, the game room.

I never went into the game room; there wasn't anyone to play with for the most part. I had placed the room in the event that I had a party or something. It had two dartboards, a pool table and a foosball table. It also had a stereo with surround sound and a big screen television that wasn't fun to use, because there wasn't anyplace to sit. When I watched movies alone, when I first got it, I used to watch them in the game room, but it got old after awhile and I had never really used it since.

I opened the door and there she was.

"Oh...my...God !!!"

There she was, laid out on the pool table, clothing gone. She was naked. She clicked the stereo remote and soft music filtered through.

"This is NOT helping the situation one bit, Maria." The pain of desire welled quickly and forcefully within me. I just stood there.

"Look, over there..." she pointed to the charcoals that lie on the table with the sketchpad on the easel.

"Where did that easel come from?" I walked to it. It had a new sketchpad on it and the charcoals were the same that I had used on the wall. "What's it for?"

"You drew that wall, right?"

I nodded. "Yes, at night when I couldn't sleep, I drew a dream I had been having and it turned out to be Jesus."

"Draw me?"

I raised a brow. "Here? Now?" I didn't know if I could do it. I hadn't drawn but for that wall in years and I always sucked at drawing faces. "I am not that good."

She sat up and folded her legs Indian style. I had to close my eyes.

"OH, sorry." She moved her legs so that I didn't have to stare quite so much. "I just want you to try. Draw me here on the pool table. I will lay and you can just play with it. It keeps us apart and takes time."

"How much time are you planning on filling? How long do we have to do this separate thing? I am not sure I can do it with you around and I don't want you to leave."

She looked at her ring, not daring to come off the table. "Did you have a date in mind?"

"I hadn't really thought about it and can't really think of anything right now, other than touching your gorgeous body. Hold on." I ran from the room and came back with a robe. "Here, you have to put this on and I will draw you on one condition...you are fully clothed."

"Chicken." She said making chicken like movements with her head. "Bok...bok...bok..."

"That's right. I am trying to do the right thing here. I have heard about you Catholic girls. Uh huh...you are rotten. Rotten to the core."

"You got that right." She moved from sitting on the table

to standing on it and made quite a production out of putting the robe on. "What time is it?"

I looked at my watch, "eleven o'clock. Why? You got a date?"

"I do, as a matter of fact. I have to watch television. You didn't like my surprise, so I am going to go watch cartoons."

She walked from the room and went to the living room and flipped on the television.

I took a very cold shower and joined her, somewhat refreshed. "You are just mean and evil." I said to her.

She grinned from the couch, still in the robe but with a throw tossed over her as well, all curled up on the couch.

"I know."

"So, where do I sit?"

"Why don't you try laying with me? We just have to let it ride and I can't help my evil twin, she gets out so little that when she's around you, I'm afraid she's merciless."

"I noticed."

"I won't tease you any more. It really isn't fair, is it?"

"I just don't want to screw up. How far is it that we can go? I mean, with lesbians, how do you tell when you've actually gone too far and call it making love?" I was curious as to her answer.

"Hmmm...I never really thought about it. I suppose if there is an orgasm involved then its probably too far. But, then again, I could orgasm with you without you touching me, if you just rubbed your leg on me, so that doesn't count. With men, it's easy to determine, penetration. Right?"

"Right. So, does that mean if you aren't penetrated, then we haven't had sex?"

"I don't know, that could mean that you could lick me and that wouldn't be sex. And, as far as I am concerned, that's the best part of sex. So, we would be wrong in that assumption."

"How about this..." I said, "If we don't touch each others... um...what's a good word here? Each other's...well, dang it, how about if we just don't *touch* each other?"

"That works for me. My girlfriends in high school they didn't have sex if they gave a guy a blowjob. But, Biblically I am not sure if a blowjob counts or not. So, since we both think blowjobs are not sex...right?"

"Right..."

"Okay then, we can give each other blowjobs, just no sex. This is ridiculous. What I really want to do is make love to you. I can't stand being this close and not being able to touch and yet, I want to honor my pledge and not touch. AND, I definitely don't want to be apart from you, so we best decide what is it the ground rules are and abide by them. I promise I won't tease you anymore like tonight." She smiled sweetly.

"You have a deal. Now, let's get to the bottom of these rules." I said as I stripped off the pajamas I was wearing and moved to take her robe off and lay on top of her on the couch. It's like that the rules were made.

Chapter Nine

Maria and I came to the conclusion that our dreams would be achieved by following solid basic groundwork and we laid that foundation early on. It had been months since we determined the rules and set a date for our holy union, May 5th. In order to uphold our vows, we had to have a solid commitment to something other than what other people thought was acceptable. We began praying together at night before bed and that is how we would fall asleep. Maria spent the week working on the deck with her friends and at night we would lay naked and watch television, never exploring or touching too much. The few times we made mistakes and ended up in different bathrooms taking cold showers separately taught us good lessons.

Maria went back home after our week and a beautiful deck completion and only spent Friday and Saturday nights at the house with Saturday day being our time together. We would go to church on Sunday's and have lunch with her family at their house. I usually spent the afternoon and from there would go home, alone, to an empty house. We never touched at all in front of the family and for the most part everyone was okay with how things were going. The only one that had a problem with things was Sarah, Maria's sister.

It was at our usual Sunday lunch that we became aware of the problem.

Sarah said, "Maria, I want to go live with you at your other house."

"What do you mean?" Maria's face immediately went blank.

We were in the middle of Sunday lunch, had been talking about whether or not to plant a garden this early or wait until June and Sarah's outburst had shut everyone up.

Sarah continued, "I want to go with you to your other house. Mama said that I could ask you to go one weekend, but I want to go today." She pouted.

Maria looked at Deidre for confirmation and Deidre shook her head yes.

"It's not my house, my other house, Sarah, it's Shane's house. I just go visit so that I can do my homework. I graduate next weekend, remember?"

Sarah whined, "But Mama said you were living there for two weeks from now." Sarah's five-year-old understanding was apparent.

"You told her that?" Maria said to her mother.

The entire room was silent.

"What am I supposed to tell her, Maria?" Deidre said. "Come help me in the kitchen...now!"

Maria got up and left the room.

Albert said to the boys, "Let's go turn on the last part of the game, she can't stop us today." They lit for the living room, which left Monica, Sarah and I.

"I'm not getting involved in this one, " Monica said.

I was left with Sarah.

"Shane, why won't they tell me why Maria is leaving me?"

"She isn't leaving you, Sarah. She's going to move out, because she is graduating and she's going to start her internship so she can be a doctor."

"But why did Mama say that she was going to go live with you and that was that and Daddy got all mad. Why is everyone fighting about Maria moving? Even Monica said that now she could do whatever she wanted, cuz Maria wasn't the little angel anymore."

"I'm sorry, Sarah. It's hard to understand, isn't it?" I held out my arms and she climbed from her chair to my lap.

"Is Maria moving?"

Maria and Deidre came back into the room, both solemn looks on their face.

"Sarah, how would you like to spend the night with Maria and Shane in Maria's new house tonight?" Deidre said.

Her eyes lit up, "Yah! I wanna go with them. Can I go pack? I can take my doll and my bear and my..." She kept going on even after Deidre said yes and all the way up the stairs she listed items she would bring.

"Are we going to need a bigger place?" I asked.

"She doesn't have to go to school until noon tomorrow. Is this okay with you, Shane?" Maria said.

"Of course it is. You have a test tomorrow morning though, don't you?" Her finals started and then graduation was the following weekend.

"I forgot. Mom, I can't..."

"It's okay, I'll take her with me. I don't have to be at work until ten tomorrow and Janie can watch her if I have a client come in. It'll be okay. I can take her to school on my lunch hour."

We left just before two and took Sarah and her bag of goodies with us to the house.

Once home the real work started. The house wasn't much by way of playful for a five-year-old, or so I thought. The first place she went was out on the back deck she had heard so much about. Maria had to make a phone call and Sarah and I ended up on the deck with Sarah.

"Let's play with my babies...k Shane?" she pulled three babies from her bag. "Here's yours, her name is Sally and here is mine. She's Frankie and here is Maria's, she is Becca. Can we make a baby bed over here?" she was pointing to the new brick fireplace we were building next to the deck.

"Sure."

"Okay, she put a couple of blankets in the fireplace and we laid the babies in it. She then went up the deck steps to the top and said she was going shopping and I had to baby sit. She disappeared up the steps. She sang a song and moved around clomping her shoes on the deck making noise while I sat down on the lower deck and watched the babies in the fireplace.

As Maria came onto the deck she said, "I think you could

be charged for child abuse. You aren't a very good babysitter. Are you sure you want children?" she laughed. Then she said, "Sarah, come get your babies, Sweetie. Shane has to do some chores around the house."

Reluctantly she trudged down the stairs, still clomping on the wood. "She was supposed to baby sit while I was shopping; I never get out of the house."

We both laughed. Maria saved me from babysitting and we went inside. Usually we worked on our projects, but not this afternoon.

Maria said, "Do you want to take her to a movie or something? How about for ice cream or to that new kids museum?"

"Why do I feel like if I say yes you are going to bid us farewell and we are on our own?"

"Because I am, I need to study. You know I have a final in Creel's class tomorrow. I can get an A if I get an A on the final and I can keep my G.P.A. It's important, Honey…just one more day, two more tests. I would have two finals in one day and none the rest of the week, just my luck."

"Are you sure she will be okay alone with me? I am more the grown-up kind of company girl. Ya know?"

"C'mon, Shane, she won't bite you. Take her to the museum and if you are good, when she goes to sleep tonight then we can lay on the couch." She raised her brow. "The evil twin is out tonight."

"Maybe I should just go to your mom and dad's for the evening?" I laughed. "I'll take her to the museum and out to that pizza place that has all the games you like for dinner. After that, I will be worn out and we are headed home."

"I love you, Shane. She will love it. She doesn't understand and I don't think that they know what to tell her. The other kids just look at it like at least they have more room in the house, but Sarah and I are very close. Mother thinks that Sarah believes that I am leaving her and that it will be extremely hard on her. I think she will be just fine, but having her over as often as possible would be great."

"I understand. It's fine. It's either go have fun with Sarah or go out and put bricks in that fireplace. I am so sore from working yesterday that I think I need a day off." I laughed again. She had worked me so hard trying to stay away from her.

"Two weeks, Baby, just two more weeks. Can you believe, after tomorrow, finals of all things, and then I have to get ready for graduation and finish my wedding plans. Did I tell you that I got my dress back Friday?"

"No and I don't want to know. Please don't make me think of you in anything but the flannel shirt and realllllly baggy jeans that I picture you in. I can barely take it as it is. Thirteen days, don't you think I know how long? I count it down. Next week I start counting hours, Sugar...hours."

"Sarah, Shane wants you to come here." She yelled out toward the back door and that was the end of our conversation.

Sarah and I had our afternoon and on the way home she fell asleep in the car. I carried her in the house, fumbling with the door until Maria came and helped me in.

With a little kiss on the check, she took Sarah from me and headed for the downstairs guest bedroom.

Sarah peeked back over Maria's arm and said, "Thank you, Aunt Shane."

I stood there in a daze...'aunt Shane?'

Maria just kept on walking, kissing Sarah on the head and shushing her back to sleep.

She returned, "Where did she get that from? Was she calling you that while you were gone?"

I shook my head, "No, that's the first I heard it. We had a great time, but she never said anything about anything. We just played. The new kids museum is the coolest. Can we go there sometime again? And, that pizza place...we ate so much and we won this big bear. I left it in the car. It took thirty dollars, but I won her the bear she wanted. She said I was her hero." I gloated.

"I bet you are, Darling. She adores you. I just don't know

where she came up with the Aunt thing." She grimaced, "Mom will just love that one."

Finals came and went and Maria planned the wedding. My input was in place, but before I could take a full week off for our honeymoon, I had to put in quite a bit of work. It was best that way; we had come close to failing in our attempts to remain celibate a couple of times. The less time we were together the better of a chance we had at maintaining our goal.

I called Maria from work, "Hey there...how are you?"

"As good as can be expected considering I get married tomorrow." She laughed. "Are you backing out on me? This is the real thing, you know?"

"I know, no way you are getting rid of me, Girl. You're stuck with me."

"Figures..." she sighed.

"Maybe I should just take your wedding present back?"

"Oh, Shane, you wouldn't...would you?" She whined.

"You better shape up and make it well worth my while." I laughed. "Hey!!! I just thought of something. Would phone sex have counted as sex?"

"Oh great, think of it now."

"We could do it right now? I could jump up on my desk and you could have your way with me." I teased. "Oh, wait, what if Mr. Parker walked in? That might not be too good, loose my chance at partner, because I am moaning too loudly in the office."

She was cracking up. "You are so bad. And, I hope you can save some of that bad for tomorrow night."

"I have been saving it for quite some time, Sugar. I think we have tomorrow night covered. But, Gary told me that your wedding night is actually the worst time to have sex. He said you are tired, worn out from all the festivities, usually have drunk too much and well, if you are driving anywhere then it's just shot to hell." I laughed.

"Trying to get out of it, are ya?" She whined again. "I knew you would be an old fuddy-dud. I should have gone with a younger model."

"You just wait..."

"What are you gonna do? You can't catch me. You can't outwit me and you can't keep up with me. You better have been working out, Old Lady. I am gonna wear you out tomorrow. I am gonna dance until you can't dance any longer and them I am gonna dance some more. And the whole time I am going to remind you that you know what I look like underneath that dress."

"You are the evil one. I called you for a reason, Miss I know it all." I could hardly contain my smile."

"I'm sorry, I thought you just missed me. What can I do for you?"

"I did miss you and that's what I called for, to tell you how much I love you and that you better be good at your bachelorette party. All those naked women, I should be so lucky. My friends are taking me out to dinner. I ammmm old." I was the one whining now.

"Are you jealous?" she chided.

"You're damned right I am jealous. I want to be with you, not some naked strippers and some straight girls. And, Kim and Randi, they will have more fun." I pouted.

"Too bad. Guess you just better deal with it." She got serious for a second. "Do you realize that I won't see you until tomorrow when we are walking up the aisle to get married?"

"I do, yes ma'am, that's why I called to tell you that I missed you. I am leaving work and going straight over to Mar's. We go to dinner from there. They said something about packing a bag, because they didn't want me sneaking away to see you."

"Sweetie, did your mom call, by chance?" She asked.

"No. I know she isn't coming. It's okay. I am fine with it."

Maria had made me call and talk to her after we sent the invitation to the union. It hadn't gone well.

Sarah came up to Maria and in the phone I heard her whine that she wanted to talk to me.

"Guess who wants to talk to you know who.' Maria kidded me.

"Put her on." I waited for her.

"Hi Aunt Shane."

"Hi, Honey. How are you today? Did you draw me another picture?"

"I drew some cats for your present. Mom told us not to tell you that we got you something, cuz we aren't going to your party, but I told her I could keep a secret. And I can, cuz you don't need to know where we put your smoker grill."

"Well, good for you. You are the best secret-keeper in the world."

We spoke for a few more minutes and then Maria got back on the phone.

"Sweetie, I have to go, I have to get this work done or we won't be having a honeymoon. I love you and am the proudest woman on earth. I can't wait to do this, to marry you."

"Twenty-one hours, Miss McAllister, and you are all mine." The passion dripped from her words and sent an electric pulse straight to my stomach.

❧

"Mar, I can't go in there." I said, looking up that sign. "It's a strip club."

"You have to, Shane."

"You told me that we were going to dinner and then we were staying in so I could relax. What is this about?"

Sherry jumped in, "If you don't go in willingly, I can make you."

She was much larger than I and could definitely be a deciding factor.

"C'mon, Shane," Mar said, "You have to do this. You only get married once. Let us have our fun."

I threw my hands up, "Okay...Okay. You win. I am going home early though."

They winked behind me as I handed the bouncer my ID.

Once inside the smoke filled room came alive. As the door opened the music filtered out into the street. It was definitely a strip club.

"Oh, my God, this is crazy." I turned around to leave only to have Sherry grab my arm and scoot me to a table near the stage.

"We reserved a table." She laughed.

The table was bigger than the three of us needed and it was almost midnight. I was so tired I could barely move. They had taken me to ten bars and I had to drink a shot at each one. My head was not clear and I just wanted my bed.

"Why so many chairs, there are just the three of us." I said over the music.

Mar yelled back to me, "Oh, we will be having company. I just saw them come in."

Towards the door I saw Randi and Kim and right behind them was Maria.

"There's Maria." My face lit up. She saw me about the same time as Kim pointed to the table.

She waved over the crowd. She had on a white skirt, gauze shirt and her hair was down. I hadn't seen her in anything but shorts and a tee or sweats for so long, we were abiding by our rules. I had worn torn jeans that were sizes too big and sweatshirts around her. We didn't need any distractions.

She came up to the table and kissed my cheek. "What are you doing here? Did you plan this?"

"No, I thought maybe you did when I saw you come in. What are they doing? Don't they know we planned to not see each other tonight?"

"I don't think they knew." She yelled over the crowd. "They drug me all over the place and then to here. I didn't want to come." She sat down in the chair next to mine.

"Me either. I about didn't come in, but Sherry threatened me."

Sherry smiled from across the table. They had met Kim and Randi a couple of times and everyone seemed to get along quite well.

"So..." Maria yelled to them all. "What are we going to do now?"

Mar helped us to understand. "See that room over there?" she pointed to a room with beaded curtains.

We nodded.

"Well, we bought you a special lap dance." They all laughed as if they knew something we didn't. "You two have an appointment in there. Figure it out for yourselves. We all chipped in."

"Yeah." Kim said, "See you later, you two go on in and have some fun."

Randi grabbed my hand and pulled me up. "Need some help getting there?"

I said to Maria, "We need smaller friends." And everyone laughed as we moved that way.

"Do you know what's going on?" Maria said.

"Honestly, I don't. And, let me tell you how afraid that makes me."

We walked into the room and inside there was a large gentleman. "You Shane and Maria?"

We nodded as Maria took my hand and stood behind me, peeking around.

"Here, let me help you. Follow me."

He led us out that door and down a long hallway. The music softened the farther down the hall we got until we were at a back door. He opened it. "Your friends got this for you."

Outside was parked a white limo. The driver saw us come out and the bouncer waved to him. "They're all yours."

"Ladies..." He opened the door to the stretch.

We climbed in. There was a note from the girls that just said, "We couldn't think of anything to do and we figured that neither of you would be much fun without the other, so take a drive, it's yours till two and...be good."

"Well, alright for them." Maria said as she settled in the seat. "Take us to the Dobey Bridge on sixty-third, please."

"What's the Dobey bridge?" I asked.

"It's a little bridge that when you go over it and make a wish, it comes true when you come back over it. I want to go make a wish."

❧

We had asked the church if they would allow us a holy union inside, but they refused, suggesting that the conflict, should someone find out, would not make for worthy news. We tried a couple of the other non-denominational churches, but really didn't have much luck. So, we approached the factory across the street from the church and rented their parking lot for the day. We could still be close to our church and for the most part, felt that we were connected in that respect.

Everything was ready: the tents were in place, the caterer's tables were set up, the cake was luscious, on time and in one piece; the stage was ready for the band and the altar was spread with flowers of every kind. The chairs for the guests were in place, divided down the middle with a red carpet and each row was separated by a silk floral arrangement. It didn't resemble a parking lot anymore, but rather, a small makeshift church. Maria and my plans came out beautifully.

I was dressing in the cafeteria of the church with Mar, Sherry and Gary. Conversing lightly, trying to keep my mind off of things and to stay free of anxiety, I almost ripped my dress trying to get it over my head. It was long and flowing made of white chiffon that molded to my curves as Maria and I had decided. We chose our dresses separately, neither wanting the other to see beforehand, but we had decided that we wanted to resemble one another in some ways. No huge trains, no messy veils, and no heels to trip over. We both chose to wear white ballet slippers and had gone to pick them out together.

I looked in the mirror, Mar behind me.

"You look beautiful." She breathed. "Let me tuck up that little piece of hair."

"Wow...Shane." Is all that Sherry could get out.

"I think this will do just fine," I said. I was impressed. Something shone in my eyes, my makeup had turned out well and my coloring was nice, even though I had actually not gotten any seep last night, Maria in my arms until she woke up and then she had left.

I glanced out the window in time to see Ed Phipps pull up with his group of followers in three vans.

"Holy hail...Ed Phipps is here." Mar said. "How did he find out?"

Ed was the local-gone-national crazy. He had once been an attorney that was disbarred by the state. Hatred was written all over his lifestyle, he'd created a church that the congregation consisted of his family members and had gone ape-crazy. His son had been ostracized by his family for being gay and Ed made his whole life a ministry of 'saving the homosexuals.' He constantly picketed churches, funerals and gay events. Their signage read things like, "God hates fagots." I couldn't believe his lack of intelligence in his crude attempt to fight back. He had made a fool of himself numerous times, all in the name of hate.

Guests were already coming and being seated and Ed and his group were tumbling out of the vans with their signs. And then I saw Mary pull up.

"Shit. Maria's grandmother came." None of the family was going to come but cousins and Rosina and Jesse that we knew of, but Deidre's mother was now getting out of a car.

Mar and I lit for the door. I grabbed up my skirt and held it as we trailed through the cafeteria to the outer door. Across the street we flew, trying to get to Mary before Ed Phipps did. We were not in time.

"You don't belong here. Take your signs and go home." Mary, standing all of four foot, eleven was saying. "How can you sleep at night?" her Spanish accent thick.

We got there about the same time, as did six of Maria's cousins and the shoving started. Mar grabbed Mary's arm as Juan pushed me backwards accidentally. He stood six-foot-six and weighed in at a mere three hundred and twenty pounds. Full of muscles and a black belt in karate, he was quiet the tower of strength opposing Ed and his followers.

"Why don you jus leaf here now?" Juan said.

"Shove it." One of the "Church-Goers" said.

"I wheel jus chove jew." He grabbed two of them at once, one under each arm and deposited them, kicking and screaming across the street at the church.

Little Miguel, at six-foot-one, two-twenty, joined in. They were taking the group across the street one and two at a time. The other four cousins just shoved them across. Mar took Mary by the hand and led her to the back of the tent.

I was left facing Ed alone with his wife. "Please don't do this, Sir." I was a little shy at first. "This is a wedding. Please don't do this."

He was haggard looking, much younger than you would believe by looking at him.

"Who the hell are you?" He asked.

"Shane McAllister, you don't know me, but I know you. Wouldn't it make more sense to join us to sit instead of fight? You can sit at the back…even keep your signs up; just don't hurt anyone else. We'd love to have you celebrate with us."

The next thing I knew the wife's fist hit me square in the jaw. I reeled backwards. She came at me again, while I stood there in my ignorance, not believing what had just happened, I took another sucker punch in the face. This time she grabbed my hair and hit me in the face a couple of times before Juan apparently came up and grabbed her. I held my face in my hands; blood was dripping everywhere. I didn't want it dripping on my dress, so I stood, bent over, trying to control the bleeding.

Mar scooted me from behind, sweeping me across the street as the police cars pulled up. It ended up a free-for-all brawl. Apparently most of Ed's group was taken to jail along with Juan. The others hadn't been taken.

Mar worked diligently to fix my face, Sherry ran for towels.

"How did this happen?" She asked. "I turned around after convincing Mary that the boys had it under control and saw that woman smack you. What did you say to her?

"All I said was that I was getting married and wanted no trouble; I invited them to join us." I laughed. "That was a big mistake."

"Ouch!!! Mar, Jesus, can't you try not to move my nose?"

She had pushed hard, "I am trying to stop the bleeding. It's already on your dress. What a lovely picture for your album."

She pointed to the bloodstains on the hemline and one big spot on my waist.

"Oh noooo...not on my dress." I whined. "Find out where they took Juan and let's go get him. Use my cell." I dug in my bag to find the phone.

"There is no way that he'll be out in time. We have to figure something else out." Sherry said.

I rolled my eyes. "Why today? Who told Ed what was going on? We didn't put anything out there to the public. I hate when he does this stuff."

"What time is it?" Mar inquired.

Gary said, "We have about ten minutes. I just checked and everything is back to normal. Is there any way we can fix her dress?"

"I don't know. At least her face is cleaned up a little." Mar said.

"Let me look in the mirror."

My face was starting to swell and I had a big purple bump right below my left cheekbone. My left eye was bloodshot and I had a large cut on the edge of my eyebrow; that is what was bleeding apparently.

"I look terrible."

"Shane, it's not something you can even worry about right now." Sherry said.

Mar chimed in, "Yeah, it's no big deal. At least everything is okay and we are still on time. And, big bonus...Ed is not there anymore."

It was time to go so we all headed out the door and back across the street. Maria was going to be driven in, because she didn't want to dress in the same place, to even take a chance of seeing each other before we walked down the aisle. Jesse was going to give her away. Even though the family accepted that we were doing this they didn't feel like it was something they could support. Deidre's exact words were, "When I tell your father he will probably have more than a hard time and I am not going to put us through that. The church made it clear, they can't support you and neither can we. We love you both, we just can't support this."

It had crushed Maria, but like she said, "You can't win them all."

I saw Jesse waiting for me and moved to where I stood with him outside the tent, awaiting Maria's arrival.

"Are you ready, Tiger." He said making reference to my eye.

I winced, "Yes. I guess I'm gonna have a pretty good shiner, huh?"

He nodded as I saw Kim's car pull up; Maria was here. She stepped out of the car in a white Elizabethan collared lace gown. It flowed long and full down her waist, fitted, to a full skirt.

"She's lovely, isn't she?" Jesse said.

I just shook my head. Her hair was up and tendrils fell down around her face. The tiara veil dropped just at her eyes and flowed down her back. I stood, unable to move, her beauty stopping me in my tracks. Jesse prodded me forward.

I took a deep breath when I saw Albert touch Jesse on the shoulder.

"I can to this, Jesse..." Albert said.

Jesse backed away, a shocked look on his face. No one had expected this.

Albert held his arm out, slightly bent and raised for me to take a hold of. "Shall we..."

I broke into a smile, "We shall."

Maria was to meet me at the aisle and that would be the first that we saw each other, but she didn't even notice me when we walked up. I saw the tears well in her eyes, but they never fell.

"Thank you, Daddy..."

We walked down the aisle on Albert's arms. He joined out hands when we got to the altar and for the first time Maria saw me. As we turned to face the minister she whispered to me.

"What happened to your face?"

I whispered back, "It doesn't matter, let's get married."

We had written our vows and pledged to each other that we would always honor and cherish our tie together and committed that day to help others to know God loved them. And, no one knew I had forgotten to put my shoes on under my dress.

Chapter Ten

The orchestra began playing and the bar opened. The guests moved to seat themselves so that they could see the dance floor and the real party started. The cake had gone well and everyone seemed quite pleased with the turn out. There were lesbians, gay men, Maria's family and some people from the church that had wandered by.

The bandleader said, "Why don't you ladies give us the first dance. Please give a warm hand to the McAllister-Sanchez ladies."

We had decided to hyphenate our names alphabetically and had instructed the bandleader for our introduction.

We walked around opposite ends of the table and met on the dance floor.

She whispered to me, "Shane, this is the happiest day of my life." She kissed my cheek and gracefully followed my lead to a two-step.

We had practiced dancing together one night, the night we almost slipped in our vow of celibacy. I danced with her easily, smelling her perfume, feeling the warmth of her body; the material of her dress was intoxicating in its own right. She was gorgeous.

"Shane..." she said again.

I looked into her eyes and immediately she marked me. She bore into me with the most passionate, hungry look she had ever given me. I wondered if she could read my mind.

"I don't have any panties on..." She said.

I swallowed hard.

"And..." she continued, not leaving my eyes, "I'm wet."

I wanted to moan in pain. I closed my eyes. She continued dancing, almost dragging me across the floor, my legs were rubber. We didn't dance closely, because we didn't want to offend anyone.

"This is the longest song I have ever heard." I croaked out, the lump in my throat pronounced.

She paid no attention to me as she smiled at guests as we danced past them. "You know," She said. "This is probably the last I will see of you for quite a bit tonight. At a Mexican dance, everyone else dances with the bride. So, I am going to be away for a while. I wanted to assure you that the red lace bra that is under this dress is just for you...and I have a red garter that you have to take off in a bit, don't go too high, we don't want anyone to see your present." She raised her brow. "Do you know what I am going to do to you later?"

I swallowed again.

"I am going to tear you up." She then growled at me.

I said nothing.

When we had chosen between the garter sale and the dollar dance, we had decided on the garter, because Maria said that it was more fun and that the dollar dance took forever. When it was time for the garter sale, the bandleader again took charge. I had hardly seen Maria; we had both been swept away with guests requesting dances. Even Kim and Randi had a dance with each of us.

"Are you ready for this?" Maria asked me as she sat down on the chair in the middle of the dance floor.

"Oh, you bet I am. I have been running this through my mind since you told me you were commando. How high up is it?"

"You think I was going to make it easy for you?"

"Maria..." I whined. Fear crept into my imagination as I pictured the garter clear up her thigh and a hundred people standing around watching me try to get it off without showing them EVERYTHING.

"I'm just kidding. It's just above my knee and I am going to cross my legs for you."

"C'mon...let's get the show on the road." Sherry yelled from her seat. Others began yelling too.

"Yeah...let's see those legs." Whistles and calls were abounding from the men.

Kim and Randi were yelling, "Take it off. Take it off."

Everyone began chanting with them as Maria crossed her legs. Slowly I lifted her dress.

"C'mon. It isn't like she is going to bite you. Take it off. Take it off."

I finally got the dress up over her knee and there it sat, the red garter.

"Let's see what you got, Shane." Someone yelled. "Get it with your teeth."

I reached to her with my teeth as she held that leg up, careful not to uncross her legs and with my teeth I grabbed the garter off and stood back up."

The audience clapped as I stood there with her garter in my teeth. I could smell her perfume on it. Through my teeth I said, "Someone is going to have to really pay for this one."

"Let's get the bidding started..." The bandleader said.

From there it was just plain fun. We said goodnight to everyone right after that and excused ourselves to leave for our honeymoon.

"Churches are spooky at night." Maria said as we gathered my things from the cafeteria where I had left my bag.

"I didn't think about the fact that things would be shut down this late. It is kind of eerie." I found a light switch and grabbed my bag so I could change into jeans. All of the sudden someone grabbed me from behind. I dropped my dress, now back in its bag, my things and screamed at the top of my lungs.

Maria laughed. "Scared ya, didn't I?"

I started to speak as she pushed me back against the wall, kissing me with the most wanton passion ever. Groping at her, I pulled her close, enmeshing our bodies. I could feel her heat against me.

"I want it now, Shane. I can't wait." She panted. "I don't want to wait."

My tongue roved her neck finding that little spot that made her moan shamelessly and she did. My stomach reacted immediately with that tug that began deep inside and sent a wave of heat up and down my body. My knees weakened as I tasted her lips again, this time not holding back. Probing with her tongue she pressed her hands on my breasts, hard and needy. She had me pinned against the wall and it felt so good. She slammed her leg against me.

"Wait..." I panted. "Wait, not here..." I slurred the words as if I were drunk. "Not here, Maria."

"I know." She slowed but didn't stop. "I know...I just wanted to feel you again. I couldn't wait any longer."

"Not in the church, definitely. " we both laughed and ran out to the car.

Maria was all over me in the car. Her hand slid between my legs the moment I started the vehicle. Her lips at my earlobe, nibbling and biting playfully, practically sitting on my section in between the seats, she slid her leg between mine and the steering wheel and the car careened as I slammed on the brakes.

"You are going to kill us both." I said. "How am I supposed to drive?"

I had to pop the lever to raise the steering wheel to prevent us from wrecking, because she wouldn't move. She purred in my ear and fondled my breasts. I was in so much pain. I hurt so bad that I thought of pulling the car over and making love to her. But, we had waited this long.

I asked her again, "How am I supposed to drive?"

"I don't know..." she kissed my nipple and continued her wanton disregard for my driving. "And...I don't care." She bit my nipple hard.

"OUCH!!!" I screamed it, but it was more a scream not to stop than it was in pain. It caught me off guard and my senses were so heightened.

"Don't you want to pull over and make love to me right here?" She was purring again.

Two could play at this game. I pushed against her until she was back in her own seat, making sure I was keeping my eye on the road.

"What are you doing?" she sounded rejected.

"Oh, Sweetie, two can play this game. You teased me so badly, now it's my turn. Just let me play. Lean back..." wicked undertones in my voice prompted her. With one hand on the wheel, I reached over with my freehand and reclined her seat; she popped backwards. Dragging my hand across her body, first at her thigh, parting her legs and caressing just above her knee and then slowly moving higher. Ever so slowly, I moved my caressing to just below the seam in her jeans. I then moved quickly to her breast and rolled her nipple between my fingers over her two shirts. It had gotten a bit chilly. I rolled her nipple, lightly flicking it and then rolling it again until she moaned for me.

She kicked her shoes onto the floor and put her feet up on the dash; covering my hand with hers, she pressed my palm against her breast, her eyes closing seductively. I slid my hand out and moved her hand back to her breast and used it to rub so that she would know I wanted her to continue, while I went elsewhere. I quickly pulled her shirt from out of her jeans and ran my fingernail up her tummy. Tensing at my touch, I noticed that she had moved her other hand to her free breast. In one she pinched at her nipple and the other she massaged. I could hardly contain myself.

I ran my hand under the waistband of her jeans, unbuttoning the top as I went. She jumped a little at my touch but settled back quickly. Zipping down slowly, I ran my hand underneath her jeans, still minus panties, and slipped my hand between her legs and we moaned at the same time. Grinding her hips against my hand I felt the soft wetness, my hand slid easily finding the three spots she loved and never staying too long on one, but moving to the others emitting more emotion from her. The dash creaked as she pushed harder against it, her polished toenails curing down to grab more of a grip.

I began to move to the rhythm of the music, classical with

long sensuous undertones. When it droned too long she would move her hips harder and moan differently, trying to lead me to her when I wasn't in the least bit interested in her orgasm. I wanted to touch.

I kept moving my hand slowly until she begged for more, getting louder than the music. Finally I gave in and made her come, pushing her feet now against the windshield to get a better position. She came hard, grabbing my arm and pulling me nearly out of the driver's seat and making me swerve yet again.

"Shane, you cheated." She said when she quit moaning so loud and calmed back down. Laying her head against my chest we drove the rest of the way; my little purring kitten sleeping soundly.

I listened to the music and thought about the night to come. Our first night together as a couple, I wanted it to be special. My dreams of making love to her had become so vivid in the last few weeks that I had awoken myself with orgasms a number of times. What would it be like to taste her again?

We pulled into the bed and breakfast at just before one o'clock and Maria said, "Oh, isn't it gorgeous?"

"It looks just like the brochures, doesn't it?" I said.

We had employed a travel agent originally to plan our trip, originally wanting to go overseas to the Orient, Australia skiing or rock climbing in the Andes...but we couldn't decide. Finally we decided to just get information on bed and breakfasts and take a more relaxing approach. It seemed more our speed. I knew all too well that the sights would go unnoticed and that Maria is all that I cared about, we decided to take a trip together at another time and to spend a quiet week together closer to home so that the travel plans didn't wear us out. Maria had to take one more test and it was a big one, so she planned to study most of the time anyway and I was planning to golf while she studied.

We were nestled at the edge of the Appalachian Foothills in Northeast Georgia. Atlanta was only ninety miles away and we truly hoped to steal a night away and to go the Peach Tree Plaza for dinner and a theatre production. A friend of mine lived in Greenville, SC and I wanted to stop and see her for a day and fish. This would give me time to have some fun and relax and Maria could sit in the sun and study. There were all kinds of possibilities.

"It suits us perfectly, doesn't it?" She asked.

A rustic mansion-type house spread out before us; the six pillar porch inviting us to enter.

"Remember the porch out back? The pictures?" I asked. She nodded. "That's what I want to see."

She didn't look like she had just woken up; she was beautiful. "It can't compare to you..." She turned and looked at me finally.

I hadn't lost my zeal for her body in the slightest; I was ripe and planning on taking care of that little problem ASAP.

She checked us in while I got the bags from the car, the gentleman owner helping me. The brochure had said they were very 'gay-friendly', and he seemed to be pleased we were there.

"I'm Tom and my wife..." he pointed inside to Maria and his wife, 'is Twila. We aint had such pretty guests in quite some time, have we Momma." He said as we approached the counter.

I had to agree with him; I felt beautiful.

They whisked us off to our room and as I was finishing up with Tom, I said, "Is it okay if we stroll the grounds this late?"

He winked at me and said, "The pool is far enough away from the house you shouldn't disturb anyone. You should be okay, but at night theys animals in the woodlands and they aren't used to being disturbed." He laughed smugly but politely and excused himself.

The moment the door closed, Maria ran forward and jumped into me, holding herself up and kissing me hard. I fell back a bit, but didn't fall down and in my thirst for her, laughing, grabbed her buttocks and slid my hand between her legs from behind.

"Honey, I have something for you...something special. I brought a little picnic, will you join me?"

"What do you have up your sleeve? Did you get me a present?" She was trying to look up the sleeve of my shirt almost knocking us over. She started tickling me, frisking my entire body as she dropped to the ground. "Where is it; I want my present."

"No...no," I hated being tickled, but she was relentless. "Stop...stop" I laughed and wiggled. "I just brought us a picnic and figured we might be hungry and..." she kept tickling me. "I brought it for us..."

"Okay, fine." She pouted. "Where is it?"

I grabbed the basket and grabbed her hand. I also grabbed a couple of towels and the complimentary robes that rested over the back of two Queen Anne chairs and said, "let's go."

Downstairs and back out to the pool we went like children sneaking, we tiptoed and giggled shamelessly as if we were doing something wrong.

We snuck out onto the back deck where there was s pal and a pool twenty feet away.

"He must not know how loud you are..." I teased.

She slapped at my arm as she magnetized herself to me from behind. The spa was enclosed on the porch, but the pool was out two French doors. I pulled my shirt off over my head and started walking forward, dropping a piece of clothing with each step: shoes, socks, jeans, panties, bra...

"You are so beautiful, Shane."

I turned around to face her and brushed my lips against hers softly, teasing her. My hands skillfully removing pieces of her clothing as I moved my lips against hers, my tongue tracing the outline, reaching for her tongue and bringing out more passion in myself, tucked away for so long. My body became alive.

I had laid the basket down as I started undressing so I pulled my lips from her and moved to grab it. She stepped out of her jeans as I was walking back her silhouette against the blueness of the pool striking.

Guiding her by the hand to the pool, I tread across the cold tile under my bare feet. We walked ten feet to the stairs that went down into the pool and as I stopped her on the third step, encouraging her to sit down as I did the same. I had no desire to speak. We had months of speaking, now it was time to let things progress even further than they had in our relationship. We had always been pressed for time in some way and now there were no time frames, no hindrances and no guilty feelings. Maria was all mine.

I laid her back, gently, on the steps feeling the warm water, the cool breeze, the contrast so vivid. Opening the picnic basket and leaning towards Maria, I kissed her and pulled my first surprise from the basket. I had made a dessert similar to the one she had made our first night together. With the ice I had packed it in, it was cold.

She leaned back on her elbows, eyes closed, the water hitting her just above the belly button. Kissing her neck, I slid my hand to her nipple and dripped a bit of the creamy dessert onto her breast and immediately sucked it off.

She gasped.

I flew to her other breast, dripping the cream again and sucking until it was gone. I dipped my finger again and dripped it between her breasts, this time letting it melt down her body. The taste of the cream mingling with her body was intoxicating. I dripped on her shoulder and licked it off then I slid my body down into the water, holding myself up with my hands on the step she was sitting on, pushing myself through the water, creating little ripples and then slammed forward, lifting myself up to her as my leg slid between hers. She wrapped her legs around me and began to slide along my thigh. I reached between us and through her wetness ran my fingers inside her. Kissing her, knowing that she would make more noise than I was comfortable with, she bit my lip. Her hips began moving wildly against me, mine in sync with her; we moved together, kissing and caressing. She dug her nails into my back as she moaned into our kiss, loudly and wildly, her head thrown back, hair falling into the water. She broke the kiss to arch her back against me she grew louder and louder. She flipped her head and half-wet hair perched onto the tile. I wanted to curl up in her hair, to lie there in comfort for a moment, too busy bringing Maria home.

She began to shudder against me. I wasn't ready – it was so quick. In her excitement, she grabbed a hold of me, her arms grabbing me and holding me close, she pushed off the steps with her feet and we careened into the water. I was still trying to move against her, my body desires more important the warmth of the water gently caressing me now. She flipped us over and pushed us back to the steps. The next thing I knew I was sitting on the steps, my knees barely covered with water and Maria was between my legs. I felt her tongue run up so fast that I screamed when it hit me. I bit my own lip, nearly drawing blood. She moved gently into a rhythm and my body began to explode; over and over, she brought me to climax. I writhed against her, holding onto her hair so that I didn't hit her too hard with my hips. I couldn't get enough of her. We made love o the steps until I could barely move anymore and then we moved to the spa, leaving the pool and its cool warmth behind.

Once in the spa, we hit the jet streams, the water pulsed against us as we lay together, spent. My eyelids were getting heavy, the events of the day becoming exhausting.

"Wanna go back to the room?" she asked.

"No, Babe, I'm fine. I would like to get out of the water though, before I slide into it and drown."

"How about that hammock over there?" She nodded in that direction. She got up and grabbed my hand and led me to it.

Butt-naked, we lay in the hammock, not a thought in the world as to where we were. We watched the sunrise and then fell asleep.

We lay together, completely spent and slept.

"Stop..." I wiggled to get away from Maria poking me. "Stop it, Maria." I didn't get to sleep on the way down here and you did." I didn't want to move and go to the room; I was comfortable where I was. And I was very whiney.

She was reluctant, poking me again. This time she spoke. "M'am, please wake up."

It wasn't Maria. OH SHIT! Before I even opened my eyes, I knew we were in trouble. It was the bed and breakfast woman, Twila. Well, so much for out good graces upon meeting I thought. I opened one eye. Sure enough, it was Twila. She stood there holding the picnic basket, which, it seemed; she had just used to collect our clothing from all over the back pool area.

There were a couple of people standing behind her watching as she tried to get us up. Then, I remembered bringing the robes down.

"Twila, can you please hand me that robe? Both of them?"

She did as I asked and we covered in them immediately. We pardoned ourselves and ran back to the room, red-faced, picnic basket in tow.

Once inside the room we threw ourselves on the bed and cracked up.

"Oh my God, I can't believe we did that." She wailed.

"I bet they were surprised to find us.. butt naked...our clothes all over the place. Two dykes asleep in a hammock, butttttt- nnnnnnaked." We roared.

Chapter Eleven

We made love again, this time in the bed roving each other bodies slowly and smoothly. She started at my fingertips and kissed and licked, in combination, stirring my inner desires again. Up my arm and over my shoulder to my neck she went, stopping at my ear and whispering, "I love you..."

She kissed my forehead, eyelids, the tip of my nose; she paid attention to every detail of my body before turning me over on my stomach. She then ran her breasts between my buttocks up to my shoulder blades and back down. I tingled at the thought as she started to do it again. Moving me to my left side, she ran her fingernail over the skin on my side, heightening my nerves and bringing me to goose bumps. She ran her tongue over my spine and down the small of my back, while she caressed my legs; I was dripping wet again.

She then positioned herself so that she had one leg between mine and she could move behind me easily. When she did move, it stirred things deep inside me; I could feel her touching me, I wanted her inside me. She moved up high enough that I could turn my head and kiss her. I couldn't stop moving her against me, groping for more leg, more skin, more Maria.

She teased me, whispering in my ear, intermittently she would moan and send me through the roof, right at my ear, so softly.

"Shane...what do you want to do today?" She could have said any number of vulgar things, but she said that...all it said to me was I am going to do to you what you have been waiting so many months for...as soon as I finish teasing you.

"Do you want to go for a walk in the woods?" She moved

her leg hard against me, sliding her hand around to my stomach and floating down...”I can make love to you under a tree, out in nature...wouldn’t that be fun?”

“Uh huh...” I mumbled.

“Wanna go play a round of golf, while I study?” She muttered again, so seductively right into my ear as her hand reached to touch me throbbing and wet.

“Uh huh...”

I had enough of the teasing. I rolled over and pulled her on top of me, “Don’t tease me anymore...please.”

“No more teasing?” she asked as she slid her finger up and over me slowly. “Are you sure?” She moved her finger quickly making me arch.

I shook my head no, as I bit my lip and watched her.

“None?” She slid her fingers inside me and moved to get her head where I wanted it, but she hung just above.

I raised my hips to make her touch me; she moved back farther...sticking her tongue out so that I was teased even more.

“No more...just touch me.”

“Touch you?” She asked, licking me once slowly. “Like that?”

“Uh huh...” I raised my hips to her again, “like that. More...”

She licked another time and flicked her tongue just a couple of times. “Is that enough?”

“No...More!” I became more urgent but I couldn’t grab her head and thrust it down, because I was holding myself up to get my hips to her.

“More, huh?” She let herself fall back on the bed, sliding her hand out and away from me. She lay there on her back and motioned with her finger, “C’mere.”

I scrambled up to the top of the bed and grabbed hold of the two posts at the top and lowered myself onto her. Immediately she began...

We stayed in bed all day, ordering in pizza and Maria studied as I slept. I was exhausted. After the wedding plans, the fight with the Phipps lady and everything else, I was just plain exhausted. I didn't feel like wandering about alone, especially after this morning, so I opted for watching Maria study and tempting her as often as I could to make love to me. Around six o'clock we were both getting a little stir crazy.

"Do we chance a restaurant?" She asked as she closed her book with finality.

I laughed. "I don't know...after last time." We hadn't been to a restaurant since Rosina drug her out and impeded upon our whole relationship.

"Let's give it a try."

We found a local restaurant that had tables overlooking a beautiful pond, entered and ordered. Afterwards we sat out by the pond and watched the sunset with our feet in the water.

"Come sit by this tree with me," she prodded me.

We sat against a tree, her back to it and I lay between her legs, quite content. The next two days were much the same, really; we spent time making love, lying in the room so that Maria could study. The wedding plans might have taken their toll on her and she wanted to make sure that they didn't affect the test.

On Tuesday I hit the golf course and left Maria to herself. Playing nine holes wore me out, but I was quite relaxed, more so than in years. It was a peaceful course and pretty much had it to myself most of the morning, not seeing another person for a couple of hours. I was rusty and shot over 85. After I finished, I went over to an area on the third hole, a water hazard I'd had trouble with. I noticed its beauty and I had about an hour before I had to be back. I wandered up to the water and walked around to a secluded area of trees. Tossing my clubs on the ground, I sat down and listened to the trees whisper. Gently the breeze blew through, touching my skin as if it were alive; I felt a oneness with nature like I used to as a child. I lay back in the grass and watched the clouds form different shapes, remembering as a child I had thought that if you wanted to you could reach up and touch the clouds.

As I reflected, I realized that I hadn't really given Maria a wedding present. It was fun going through a list of possibilities. Finally deciding what I would do, I reluctantly left the trees, the quiet and the calm, but I missed her. I'd have to bring her here sometime; it was too beautiful to keep to myself.

When I got back to the room Maria was asleep on her books. She must have fallen asleep studying. I took our camera out of the case and quietly focused on her face and shot a whole roll of film, making sure I had the book in the shot and the way she laid on it.

Playfully she came at me. I fell to the floor laughing with her on top of me. Instantly we were entangled; she ripped my shorts off, sliding her hand up my shirt. Before I knew it my bra was off and her hands were on my breasts, massaging firmly. She was moving with me, crushing me under her body weight as I kept taking pictures of her. She peeled the rest of my clothes off as I snapped pictures from any angle, reloading the camera she began to shed hers...more dramatically. I snapped away.

"God, you are so beautiful." I said to her as I moved so I could photograph my striptease.

After we made love, I took her outside to show her what I had gotten her. It was late afternoon when we walked out and there, in the parking lot, hooked to the back of my car on a trailer was a twenty-two foot, twelve man boat. She ran to the boat and slid her hands over the bow, turned to me in awe.

I said, "It's like owning three boats in one – the towing of a runabout, the roominess and amenities of a pontoon, all wrapped in the cruising and socializing of a deck boat. A 210hp M2 Jet Drive supplies power. Everything on this boat was designed for comfort and luxury, from the convenience center to the aft bench seat that converts to a sun pad lounge area." I was motioning to the boat like the showroom attendant had to me when I bought it. I swung my arms around and mocked him further, "Standard amenities include CD player; bimini top; full-size, stand-up changing room with portable head; companion seat at the helm; and a spacious bow to stern floor plan. If it's entertainment on the water you seek, look no further – your private, bloating island has just arrived. And, I am included in the package, naked on the sun pad."

"Can we afford this?" She was completely serious.

I hadn't really thought of the fact that we had never discussed finances. I shook my head in affirmation.

"We are fine, financially. I've saved most of my earnings for quite some time; I'm actually paid quite well. I paid off my house in five years and purchased my Harley with cash; I work on a cash basis most of the time, Honey. I wrote a check for the boat and will have the funds transferred from one of my liquid asset accounts when we get back. I called the bank and told them about it already. It's okay, Sweetie."

"Shane..."

"Maria, really, it's okay. I know that you have always said that you wanted to pay for your own education and all, but we are fairly well off. I've been with the firm long enough that we don't have to worry. I've invested wisely and well, I never really had extravagant needs or wants. I got a great deal on this boat; it's a showroom model from last year. I made him cut three thousand dollars off the price, just because other people have looked at it. I wanted to give you a wedding present."

She had such a sad look on her face. She came close but didn't kiss me; she just folded up in my arms.

"Shane...I can't get you anything."

"Oh, Maria. I didn't mean it that way. I can take it back, if that's what you want. I'm sorry. I didn't want you to feel bad. I will do whatever you want me to."

She held me closer. "Well, we did just get married, didn't we? And that means what is mine is ours and what is yours is ours." She acted like she was in deep thought before a huge grin came to her face. "I never really thought about it like that. We had such a hard time with everything that I really didn't think about money. We are okay?"

I nodded. More than okay, fairly well off and in comparison to what she had been, rich.

"Then…I suggest," she was playing with e now, "you must plan to take me for a spin. Can we go boating tomorrow? Is there anywhere nearby?" She was elated.

She threw her arms around me and hugged me tight.

"You got it. Do you have much more studying to do, miss-I-fell-asleep-instead-of-studying? I can check out the Internet tonight in the den or we can just go to South Carolina; I can call Victoria and see if she is free."

"That would be great."

Chapter Twelve

We got up early in the morning to what was supposed to be a beautiful day. It was in the high eighties so we packed a picnic lunch and took our champagne we hadn't used yet and headed out for South Carolina, a two-hour drive. I called Victoria and told her to meet us at the lake around noon; she gave us directions to where she would be. That would give us plenty of time on the lake alone to break in the boat.

We got there about nine thirty and loaded the boat. I had boated with Jay, so I knew pretty much what to do, even though I hadn't ever owned a boat before. We headed out onto the lake slowly; the motor purred. With a 210 hp motor, when I hit the throttle, we flew through the water. It almost scared me, threw Maria onto the floor, but we both laughed.

"Ummm...maybe you should let me drive this thing." She laughed as she got up.

"I'll tone it down a bit. Let's just cruise for a bit."

We sat in the captains seat together, even though it was big, the boat rocked. Maria wouldn't keep her hands off me; our bikinis donned, it was quite easy access. She kept putting her hand behind her, between my legs, under my bikini and immediately center. Finally, I gave up and coasted into a cove. I tossed the anchor and Maria and I made love on the water.

"Can you grab some sunscreen for me, please? I'm starting to burn."

Maria grabbed the lotion and since I was already naked, she applied it generously. Her hands on my back were turning me on again. Her abilities at massage were tremendous.

"Where did you learn to massage?"

"Actually at school. They had a class at night at school and I thought it might come in handy in my practice. I went to it for eight weeks and we practiced on each other and had all the finer training. This guy was good."

"I bet he was." I laughed and she smacked me.

"I don't know about that, but I do know that every time he wanted to demonstrate something he would call me to the front." She laughed.

"Awww, did he have a little crush..." I teased.

"He must have. It was right before I met you...Let's take a swim. Do we have time?"

I glanced at my watch, we really didn't. "Not really, Sugar. We need to get clear back to where we started from and I might have to get a map out. I'm not sure where we are really. I think we just need to head that way." I pointed, laughing.

"Oh, great. Get us out in the wilderness and lose us."

I started the engine and we scooted back across the lake. I'd been right, it was straight across the lake and relatively easy to find. We could see it from the main part of the lake. We pulled into the marina and docked. Maria went inside to get some substantial lunch; I was starving. She brought back bean burritos from a microwave, chips, salsa, bananas and some soda. We ate while we waited. Out of the corner of my eye, I saw a boat coming off the water into the marina traveling much faster than necessary.

I turned back to Maria; sitting in front of me once again and asked for the soda we were sharing. As she handed me the soda, I heard the boat motor from behind me, it was extremely loud and not shutting down as it should, pulling to the Marina. I started to stand up, making sure that if the boater needed it, we could help out. Maria climbed up at my request, my hands on her back and I turned just in time to see that there was no driver. The boat was headed directly for the Marina, namely our boat.

I screamed, "Maria, jump!!!" The boat was not ten feet away when I aw Maria turn in time to see and clear the side of the boat and jump in the water. I had more-or-less pushed her into compliance and over the side and into the water out of danger she went. I was on my way, all I heard was a huge crash and I felt myself being propelled toward the Marina building. I put my arms out and curled into a ball. I hadn't made the jump in time. "Holy Fuck!!!" in my head, I was clearly seeing that I was going to hit that wall with the force that the boat caused me to gain and it wasn't going to be good. I saw Maria watching from the water. Screaming...Maria was screaming...

I woke up dazed. Everyone was saying my name. I couldn't really tell what had happened, but my head hurt really badly. I could smell gas and it was making me sick.

"My head, Maria..." I slipped back out.

"Shane, Baby, talk to me again..." I could hear her very far away. I could feel her leaning over me bawling. "Shane, say something." She was begging.

I couldn't say anything. I couldn't feel my body. I couldn't get to her as I felt myself sucked back into the vacuum.

I tried to tell her I was okay, tried to reach up and touch her face. I could see her now as I floated out and away from her. "Maria..." I reached out. That damned vacuum again.

"Shane, Baby, talk to me..." She patted my cheek. She looked terrible.

"Hi, Honey." I reached up to touch her face. That's when I noticed that my arm was in a cast. "What the hell?" I looked. I had a cast on both arms, my leg and my ribs and my head hurt really bad. I tried to get up. "Maria..." I was afraid.

"It's okay, Sweetie. It's okay now." She started crying. "It's okay." She kissed my face softly, stroking my cheek.

"Hey there, girl." Victoria was standing on the opposite side of a hospital table. I was apparently in an emergency room.

"Hey…" I hadn't seen her for so long, but I knew that voice. I smiles, a weak smile, but I smiled. "I hurt all over…"

"You gave us quite a scare there. You're pretty lucky. I saw what happened and yanked you off that Marina before the fire started." She said.

She was a police officer, so whatever happened, she must have had a handle on it.

"Oh, wait…" I began to remember what happened. I turned to Maria. "Are you okay?" I couldn't see any casts or bandages.

"Sweetie, you pushed me overboard and with the exception of this bruise," she showed me a nasty bruise on her leg, "where I hit the side of the boat and fell over. I'm fine." She smiled. "You hit the Marian wall when the boat hit ours. It caught ours from underneath and somehow threw you forward." She began crying, this time sobbing. She put her hand sin her face and sat on the chair behind her next to the table, laying her head next to me as she cried.

"I can't reach you." I said frustrated at the casts on my arms.

Victoria came around the table and comforted Maria as she spoke to me. "Darlin', you're lucky to be alive. I don't know how you did it, but I had pulled up just as the boat came into the cove. I screamed and ran for you. That thing came up under your boat and really just pushed the boat up and over. A million other things could have happened and you would have been dead. But, it pushed you forward with such a force; you flew through the air. I saw you push Maria over the side and start to go yourself you just didn't make it. You were airborne when your boat sort of helped you clear all the mess and fly free of the two boats. You hit a part of the marina that the guys were inside working on. They had plans to make another entry door from that side and had broken away most of the wall inside; that saved your life. You fell through the wall, breaking your fall. Somehow, Sweetie, you were blessed." She winced, "You boat…now that's a different story.

The doctor came into the room just then. "Miss…" he was talking to Maria who was calming some. "I just got the X-ray and the lab back. It seems like she is fine." He then turned to me. "Well, hello there. Seems you gave us quite a scare there and your...uh...wife helped you out a bit." He was checking my casts. "You have no compound fractures, although you banged up the left side here pretty good and from what they tell me, your boat...well, she didn't fare as well." He winked.

"So, everything came back well?" Maria asked through small tears now.

"Yes. She has a slight concussion, causing the in-and-out there, and the left arm broken in three places and the right just at the wrist. Her leg is broken in two places both below the knee, one in each bone and that rib; that might be some trouble for her comfort. Other than that, I just want to make sure her head is okay. I want to admit her and run some tests tomorrow morning. I put a walking cast on, your...uh...friend, she insisted and swore she wouldn't let you use it until you get home and get your personal physician to okay it. Other than that, you seem to be a very lucky lady." He smiled as he left the room, notating the chart before he went.

The next day I got to go home. Maria stayed with me at the hospital all night and Victoria went back to the B&B and got our things for us. She took a couple of days off to help around the house and get us through Maria's test. At that point we would be home free.

Upon our arrival home, a very long trip in casts it was even though Maria let Victoria drive our car and rented an SUV with lots of room. The house was filled with family and friends and from those that couldn't make it the house was filled with flowers and balloons. Uncle Jesse carried me to the guest bedroom that Rosina had turned into a recovery room, the big screen television from the game room completing it.

As we passed the hallway that had my picture of Christ on the wall, I swear he winked at me, "Maria...did you see that?" She had to have seen.

"What, Sweetheart?" She was looking around.

"Never mind...it was nothing." I couldn't explain, but I knew I had been blessed.

Epilogue

Maria passed the test with flying colors and accepted a full-time internship with Dr. Hugo, remaining at the hospital in town. Two years later, she became Dr. Maria McAllister-Sanchez, Pediatrician. At the end of that summer we brought our first child into the world, Kennedy Jordan McAllister. She was born with Maria present, my biological birth. Maria helped me through the pregnancy: the grumpy days at the office, my horrible morning sickness, which lasted three months; the bloating and cramping and all the joys of birthing. Kennedy weighed 7 lbs. 4 ounces and had jet-black hair and blue eyes, contrary to my coloring. We had used Maria's friend, Claude, a Spanish man's sperm and Kennedy had coloring much closer to Maria's than mine, but had my eyes.

As Kennedy grew and neared two, her coloring was almost the same. She had the darkest hair and lashes and the lightest blue eyes and skin. She had my demeanor and Maria's temper. Our next child came a month after Kennedy turned two. We adopted an African- American baby from an agency a couple of states away. We found in attempts for Maria to get pregnant, that she was unable to have children, a devastating blow to not only her, but to her parents as well. We worked through it and found that one of her ovaries did not function and the other didn't release eggs, as it would normally do. All in all, we decided that our children were both gifts and we didn't care where they came from.

Elijah Adam was different than Kennedy, where she was soft-spoken and temperamental; Eli just told it like it was. He started out bold and remained that way. There wasn't a doubt in our minds that he wanted a bottle, or that he needed his diaper changed. Eli was such a joy in his exploration of the house.

We had purchased a six-bedroom house, central to my office, the best school in town as well as Maria's clinic. Eli found it his job in life to work out all the kinks in our baby-proofing the house. If we neglected to get it proofed, Eli found it. We hired a nanny, Gretchen, and life was much easier. Instead of taking the children to Deidre, as we had, we found Deidre enjoyed coming to the house much more, when she could come and go as she pleased. She would take the children on outings and give Gretchen a well-deserved break. Having an attorney and a doctor in the house left us for not much downtime. We made sure that Sunday's were committed to the family and that evening were our time with the children. Parenthood was enjoyable and our careers were diligently to aid others; we knew and appreciated the gifts we had been given. Each day we thanked God for our gifts and granted Him the appreciation He deserved.

Life wasn't always easy and Maria and I had our moments. We fought in a good way, though, ending in communication where it might not have started. Our worst fight came about one day that Maria got called into work in the middle of the night; she was on call. She didn't get home until almost eight in the morning. It was Gretchen's day off and Deidre was running late. I had a big case coming up and was in the middle of depositions. I was running late, trying to get the kids fed. Kennedy was almost four and Elijah was a mess. He was running all over the house, juice flying on the hardwood floors and I was about to lose my mind. To my despair, I sat down and cried. I hadn't slept well with Maria gone all night and we had been up late making love. For her to be called in and taken away from me right after lovemaking; it was sort of depressing. I'd lie there quietly, trying to get some sleep, but worried instead. I worried about the case, about the kids, about all kinds of things; I felt a little off-balance.

While I was crying, Kennedy brought me a glass of water. "Here is what Mama does for me when I cry, Mommy." She sat beside me on the floor, where I had regressed to and cradled my hand in hers.

She sang a song to me that Maria sang to her and then got up and held my head to her bosom.

"You're an amazing child, Kennie." I cried harder.

It seemed we never got enough time together. The clinic that Maria worked in was adjacent to the hospital and did profound research in early childhood diseases. She was a doctor; I knew that her schedule would be rough. But, I was almost forty years old now and I wanted my family time. She was just in her early thirties; maybe I was hitting menopause early? I thought.

Maria walked in and started yelling at Elijah, "Elijah, you need to stop making messes."

Eli was immediately in tear. He and Maria had an understanding; they were soulful, more so than even Kennedy and I were. He flew into the kitchen in a rage of tears and began blaming Kennedy. That started Kennedy, the little mother, off and running. Before I knew it we were all in tears, but Maria. In walked Deidre.

Immediately Deidre began screaming that the children needed a more stable environment at home and that one of us should quit our jobs, put our careers on hold. We needed a stay at home mom. It seemed to her that with two moms at least one of us should be at home with the children. Maria began to cry as well.

It was a wretched mess. The entire family was in tears, Kennedy and Elijah trying to out cry each other, reaching decibels unknown to man. Maria quietly sobbed in a corner of the kitchen and tears just streamed down my face...my poor, poor family.

In the middle of everything, the phone rang. Maria immediately went into protect the family mode. "Don't answer it, Mother." Deidre had started for the phone.

Confused and unaware that Maria had no tolerance for phone calls before nine o'clock, it was our early morning meditation time. Lately we hadn't even gotten it, someone from the children's pre-school determined to have us volunteer had called each morning the last three mornings.

"Honey, let her answer it." I said.

That was the wrong thing for me to say. The look she shot me, right before she shot the same look to Deidre could have turned me to a pile of ashes.

Maria picked the phone up herself, "Hello." She was almost rude in her exhaustion.

"No, this is Maria, can I help you?" She hesitated and then continued. "I called, because I am bleeding." She put her hand over the receiver, "Mother, can you take the children into the other room?"

Deidre did immediately.

Maria spoke back into the receiver, "I have been for about four hours and I'm cramping." She turned her back to me and moved around the corner to finish her conversation.

I had heard enough. I got to my feet and motioned Deidre to hurry. I went to Maria's side and put my arms around her and smoothed her hair back into the hair tie she was wearing. I listened as she told the doctor that she had been bleeding since we made love the night before, how she explained that it had been gentle lovemaking and that there was no reason that she should be bleeding. She made an appointment for that morning in an hour.

She turned to me, "I don't know what's wrong with me, but I'm scared."

We had been doing In-Vitro therapy attempting to get her pregnant, but had stopped months ago with no success.

"I shouldn't be bleeding, Shane."

I stroked her hair and assured her it would be okay by taking her into my arms and resting her head on my shoulder.

"Let's just go see what it is. Let me call Janie and have them get the depositions with out me." I held her for a few more minutes. She just stood in my arms.

We gathered our things and told Deidre we would be back as soon as possible. I knew there was a chance of Maria being admitted; they had done that one time prior when she had bled from the In-Vitro process. If she was worried, there was something to be worried about.

In the car we spoke very little. I finally decided to just ask her about it, "What do you think is wrong?" I flinched at the thought of the answers.

"Well, I started bleeding right after I got to the hospital. I monitored it for an hour or so, thinking that maybe your fingernail got me or something...but I couldn't remember any pain. I called this morning after it didn't stop and I started cramping. I have to be honest with you..."

Honest with me? What wasn't she honest about?

Suddenly she grabbed her abdomen and bent forward in the seat. "Shane, something's not right."

I sped up and ran two red lights to get her to an emergency room.

Maria was still bent over, cramping heavily, tears in her eyes she grabbed my leg and squeezed hard.

"We're almost there, Honey. Just hold on a little longer." I whipped into the ER and slid to a stop.

I ran around the car and helped her in: the orderly met us with a wheelchair.

Finally the doctor came in.

"Well, Maria, I see that they have done the initial tests and things look okay, but I have a hunch on this one. Let's get some tests real quick." He left the room.

"Shane, I didn't tell you something..." She looked heartbroken, forlorn.

"What is it, Maria?" I was scared.

"I had an In-Vitro session a couple of weeks ago and I went alone. I got tired of you getting your hopes up, so I went by myself. I haven't been able to live with this lie and I just feel horrible." She watched for a reaction.

"I don't understand what that means?"

"I could be miscarrying..." She started crying. "I didn't

think it worked, but what if it worked and I am losing our baby?"

"Oh, Honey…" I kissed her forehead. "Let's just see what the doctor says. We will take what he says and go from there."

An orderly entered. "Come with me Dr. Sanchez." And escorted her out of the room.

She came back into the room and the doctor came with her. "Let's get you on the table and see what we can find." He and I helped her up on the table about the time she threw up all over the floor.

"Ummm…someone, help her." She was retching all over the place.

"It's okay, Shane, just take a seat right here and hold her hand." He handed her a pan. "How long since you kept anything down?"

"Three days. The bleeding since last night…" she was calming down and laid on the table. "I don't know what's wrong, but I am nauseas and weak. My legs are made of lead; they feel so heavy. And, I'm not bleeding like menstrual cramps, not that steady, but heavier than spotting." She squeezed my hand.

An hour later he came back in. "I want to check two more things. Are you feeling better?"

She nodded.

"Why don't you go over to the coffee shop across the street and get some juice. I am going to send this lab work down and no sense in you waiting here. I will call to have you come back over."

We agreed and left. At the coffee shop my phone rang a half hour or so later, it was Deidre. Carl had called and wanted us to give him a call at his office, not go back over to the hospital. Deidre said, "Shane, he said it was damned important and he wanted to talk to you and not Maria."

My body jumped with fear, tensed immediately. I was terrified and trying not to let it show in my face. No…nothing could be wrong with her. I fumbled to dial the number.

"What is it, Shane? Who was that?" she was demanding.

I continued to dial. She grabbed my leg so hard it hurt. "What is it, Baby?"

I had to see for myself first. Then and only then could I handle it.

"Shane...I want to know."

"Hello, this is Shane McAllister..."

"Let me put you through" the receptionist said.

Carl came on the phone..."Shane...how are you and Maria doing?"

What the hell? What was he doing?

"We're at the coffee shop across the street. What is it, Carl? What is the problem?" I couldn't wait and couldn't pretend to him that I could.

"Well, Shane...you are going to be a mommy." He was laughing. "Go celebrate with our new Mommy-to-be. She isn't sick; she's pregnant with our baby. She is just spotting probably. I want her in bed today, plenty of rest, but all the same, I want her in bed. Come back next week for a regular exam, if there are no more problems. And, Shane...don't forget, she is sitting there beside you," he laughed again, "Might wanna tell her too."

She was staring at me, ashen with worry. She looked ten years older.

"You got it, Carl." I hung up the phone.

"Shane, you can tell me. I'm ready. I can handle it. What is it?" Her mind was clicking ninety-to-nothing.

I took her hands in mine, from where we were sitting in the middle of a coffee shop on a busy morning; I cradled her face in my hands and I looked into her amazing brown eyes with as much love as I had for her and said, "Baby...you're going to be a Mommy. You're carrying our baby." My smile lit up the room.

It took her a minute to catch up.

She frowned and then looked down. For a minute I thought I was going to have to tell her again. Then she looked up. All the sudden she caught up; placing her hand on her belly she said, "I am? Our baby?"

I nodded.

"Can we go tell the children?" Then another frown came. "Wait, is the baby okay?"

"You need complete bed rest and then we have some tests next week. But, he doesn't seem to think there is a problem."

At home Maria took Deidre out back while I made us lunch. You could hear the screams for blocks and Deidre came rushing back in the house.

"Shane," she said, "I'm going to be a grandma." She was gurgling. "I mean, I know I have grandkids, but..." She stammered.

"It's okay, Deidre, I understand. Congratulations."

"And, you, Shane, a mother again. How wonderful. I have to go tell Albert. Oh my Lord, we are going to have another baby." She grabbed each of the kids and gave them big kisses as she grabbed her things and headed for the door. In mid-flight she stopped and turned, just at the hallway. "You get in that bed like the doctor said and if you have any problems with her, Shane, you just call me." She grinned and ran.

We sat the table for lunch and sat down. The first thing we did, which was routine for us was to take hands and begin our meal prayer.

Maria led, "Dear, Sweet, Lord...we have been blessed in this life. Thank you for all you have given us and what you have not; the lessons you teach us and all that we are. In your glory and honor, we promise to do our best to uphold your commands to love one another and to love You more than we love anything else. I want to thank you for the special gifts you have given Shane and I, our three precious children, our home..." Maria trailed off as Kennedy spouted.

"Mama, we only have two babies, me and 'Lijah. You cannot tell God we have more, cuz He would already know. He can count pretty good." We all laughed a little.

I took Kennedy on my lap and saw Maria reach for Elijah and take him out of his highchair.

"Ken, Honey, Mama and I have something to tell you and Elijah; we're going to have another baby. Mama has a baby growing in her tummy."

Kennedy was a little confused, "But Mommy, Mama didn't

have 'Lijah grow in her tummy? We picked him out at the hospital, 'member?" She had remembered the day we picked Elijah up in Boston.

"Well, Kennie, remember when I told you that you grew in my tummy? This is the same. 'Lijah is special too, just like you; but this baby is going to grow in Mama's tummy. Remember I told you that we went to the doctor, because Mama wanted to have another baby and we prayed to God that maybe we could?"

Kennedy looked straight up at the ceiling and yelled, "Thank YOU, GOD!!!"